PRAISE FOR THE [

Here are some of the over 100,000 five star reviews left for the Dead Cold Mystery series.

"Rex Stout and Michael Connelly have spawned a protege."
                                    AMAZON REVIEW

"So begins one damned fine read."
                                    AMAZON REVIEW

"Mystery that's more brain than brawn."
                                    AMAZON REVIEW

"I read so many of this genre...and ever so often I strike gold!"
                                    AMAZON REVIEW

"This book is filled with action, intrigue, espionage, and everything else lovers of a good thriller want."
                                    AMAZON REVIEW

BLEED OUT
A DEAD COLD MYSTERY

BLAKE BANNER

RIGHTHOUSE

Copyright © 2024 by Right House

All rights reserved.

The characters and events portrayed in this ebook are fictitious. Any similarity to real persons, living or dead, is coincidental and not intended by the author.

No part of this book may be reproduced in any form or by any electronic or mechanical means, including information storage and retrieval systems, without written permission from the author, except for the use of brief quotations in a book review.

ISBN-13: 978-1-63696-023-4

ISBN-10: 1-63696-023-5

Cover design by: Damonza

Printed in the United States of America

www.righthouse.com

www.instagram.com/righthousebooks

www.facebook.com/righthousebooks

twitter.com/righthousebooks

DEAD COLD MYSTERY SERIES
An Ace and a Pair (Book 1)
Two Bare Arms (Book 2)
Garden of the Damned (Book 3)
Let Us Prey (Book 4)
The Sins of the Father (Book 5)
Strange and Sinister Path (Book 6)
The Heart to Kill (Book 7)
Unnatural Murder (Book 8)
Fire from Heaven (Book 9)
To Kill Upon A Kiss (Book 10)
Murder Most Scottish (Book 11)
The Butcher of Whitechapel (Book 12)
Little Dead Riding Hood (Book 13)
Trick or Treat (Book 14)
Blood Into Wine (Book 15)
Jack In The Box (Book 16)
The Fall Moon (Book 17)
Blood In Babylon (Book 18)
Death In Dexter (Book 19)
Mustang Sally (Book 20)
A Christmas Killing (Book 21)
Mommy's Little Killer (Book 22)
Bleed Out (Book 23)

Dead and Buried (Book 24)
In Hot Blood (Book 25)
Fallen Angels (Book 26)
Knife Edge (Book 27)
Along Came A Spider (Book 28)
Cold Blood (Book 29)
Curtain Call (Book 30)

ONE

"I've been interested in this one for a while," I said, and looked across at her. She had both elbows on her desk, which abutted mine, and her cheeks squashed between her fists as she stared at the screen of her computer.

"Uh-huh..."

I waited. Eventually the silence encroached on her, as it was meant to, and she shifted her gaze to frown at me.

"What?"

I waved the file at her. "I am going to tell you from the beginning, so be patient and listen."

She sighed and flopped back in her chair. I said, "Sadie Byrne, nineteen years of age..."

"How long ago?"

"Fall of 2018, late September, listen. Try not to talk." She sighed again and crossed her arms. I went on. "Okay, so Sadie Byrne starts to become depressed..."

"Being nineteen will do that to you."

"Be quiet, Dehan. She starts to become depressed. So much so that her parents eventually take her to the doctor, who refers them to a psychiatrist. After a few visits, when Dad goes to collect her—"

"From the shrink?"

"Yes, from the psychiatrist, Dad goes to collect her and . . ." I scanned the page for the name. "Dr. Shaw asks him to come into her office with Sadie. It turns out she has been raped."

Dehan winced. "How long before?"

"About four months prior, though she refuses to state an exact date. Thing is, she also refuses to name her rapist, or even specify how or where it happened." Dehan interjected a skeptical grunt. "Meanwhile, Dr. Shaw, who seems to be no slouch, noticed that Sadie was not looking too healthy. It might be her depression, or it might be something else. So she sends her for blood tests."

"Dr. Shaw is a woman, right?"

I glanced at her. "Yeah. Why?"

She shrugged. "She's intuitive. So she sent her for blood tests, what happened? She was pregnant?"

I shook my head. "No, she was HIV positive, and it had developed into AIDS."

She sat forward, and her eyebrows arched. "In *four months*?"

"Yeah. A very small percentage of people are termed rapid progressors, and in extreme cases can develop from contracting the virus to death in as little as a year. This was Sadie's case. A combination of poor diet, depression, lack of exercise, and a refusal to take antiretroviral medication meant she died roughly a year after her alleged rape."

She was frowning at me. "But you know that doesn't constitute murder, right? Knowingly infecting somebody with HIV is a misdemeanor in New York. In Iowa I think they take 'em out and shoot 'em like dawgs, but here in civilized New York it's a misdemeanor, unless you can prove cruel intent and a depraved state of mind. I forget the exact wording."

I nodded patiently. "I know . . ."

"And rape? We have never investigated a rape *per se*. We've always looked at homicides. Rape is *real* hard to prove as a cold case, Stone. Especially if the victim is dead *and* didn't report it at the time. How long did you say? Four months!"

"You done?"

"Yeah."

"Then sit back and listen, like I told you from the start."

"Okay." She sat back and laced her fingers over her belly.

"The curious thing is that this case cross-references to another case."

"What case?"

"Chuck Inglewood . . ."

"Rings a bell. Stabbed to death? Weird circumstances?"

"If you'll stop talking, Motor Mouth, I'll tell you. His wife, Angela Inglewood, was visiting with neighbors in the afternoon. Chuck, who was apparently not great at socializing, stayed home. According to Angela, as he was at home and it was afternoon, she left the French windows open, presumably onto the backyard. While she was having coffee with her neighbor, one Violet Nowak, she heard her phone ringing, but it stopped before she could answer it. She checked and saw that Chuck had tried to call her a total of six times. She tried calling him back but without success. The number was engaged. So she made her apologies, collected her things, and hurried home, about a hundred yards or so down the road.

"She entered the house, called him, got no answer, and eventually found him upstairs in their bedroom. He had been savagely attacked, cut with a knife, very deep wounds in his underarms and the insides of his thighs. He had bled profusely. His cell was in his right hand, and he had apparently called 911 because the cops and an ambulance showed up a minute or two later."

She had been nodding while I spoke. Now she said, "Yeah, I remember. Who had that case? Reynolds?"

"Reynolds and Hogben."

"That was a weird case. Absolutely zero forensics, no motive . . . So how does it cross-reference to Sadie Byrne?"

I shrugged. "When I say it cross-references, what I really mean is that I have found a connection. Nobody else has until now. Only me."

"Hey, Stone." She said it in a flat monotone. "You're brilliant. You know, maybe I don't tell you often enough. You're brilliant, Stone, you're brilliant . . ." Mo, across the aisle, groaned. She ignored him. "So how are they connected?"

"Chuck Inglewood was Sadie Byrne's uncle by marriage."

"Holy cow . . ."

"See? I told you. It's interesting. Cathy Byrne, Sadie's mother, was Angela Inglewood's sister."

"Are we seeing a hint of a motive here?"

I dropped the file on the desk and spread my hands. "That Chuck raped his niece and either Patrick or Cathy Byrne found out and went around and killed him? It's possible, but at this stage there is zero evidence to support such a theory."

She stuck out her lower lip and nodded. "Then again, somebody wanted to kill him. If they wanted to kill him, they had a motive. No motive was ever established, and yet . . ."

"We'll put it in the possible pile."

"Okay, so let's go see what else we can find. Where do you want to start?"

I pointed at her computer. "While you were staring at the screen of your diabolical machine, I called Angela Inglewood and asked if we could go and see the house. She said she didn't live there anymore. She'd moved out almost immediately after the murder, locked the place up, stayed a couple of months with her sister, and then bought a house in Throggs Neck."

"Huh . . ."

"But she said if we want to, we can collect the key from Mrs. Nowak and have a look around."

She nodded for a bit. "What was I doing?"

"Staring at your computer screen. It's an affliction that affects some people your age."

I stood and grabbed my jacket. She watched me and said, "What? Sorry. I was staring at my screen and I didn't hear you."

As we passed Mo on the way out he muttered under his

breath, "Jaysus! Curdle a guy's breakfast. Don't hurry back, will ya?"

It was a warm afternoon. The leaves on the plane trees on Story Avenue were still young and fresh and green, but the sky was losing that freshly washed look that belonged to March and April and had acquired that fresh, sun-and-wind-dried look that belonged to May and June.

We climbed into my ancient, burgundy Jaguar, rolled down the windows, and fired up the big engine. The cat growled its way down to White Plains Road, with the wind whipping Dehan's hair across her face, and we turned left and north to pass over the Bruckner Expressway. Along the way, Dehan shook her head and drummed her fingers on the open window. Finally she held out her hand, palm up, like Hamlet holding up Yorick's skull.

"She leaves the house, she locks it up and never goes back, she moves to Throggs Neck and buys a *new* house, but she never sells the old one."

I made a slow shrug. "Never . . . We're talking about maybe eighteen months."

She grunted. "Did she put it on the market?"

"I don't know yet. What are you driving at?"

"I don't know." She raised her open right hand again, like she really wanted me to look at Yorick's skull. "This is an odd case, so I am trying to question the things that seem most odd. And it seems odd to me that she would just walk away from the house and buy a new one, without trying to sell the old one."

"That's true." I glanced at her. "But it's not, on the face of it, the behavior of someone who is trying to conceal evidence."

She stared at me without expression, nodded, and looked out of the window. "No," she said. "It's not."

I turned right onto Virginia, and then right again onto Haviland, and stopped outside a large, two-story house set back from the road among its own lawns, with an independent double garage in back. The lawns were overgrown, and what had once been flower beds bordering the house were now more like neglected burial mounds for very small people. I climbed out of the car and walked around to rest against the far side of the car, looking up the concrete driveway toward the double garage. Dehan came and stood next to me.

"They weren't poor. What did he do?"

"He was a plumber. That's to say, he had a plumbing business. Employed a handful of guys and ran a plumbing supplies shop."

She nodded sagely. "People joke about it, but it's true. Lawyers, dentists, and plumbers."

I pointed along the drive. "Unusual."

"What is?"

"People usually have their French windows in back, so you can open them onto the lawn. This guy has his at the side of the house, leading onto a concrete driveway and his garage."

She took in what I was saying, gazing up the drive, then stared at me. "Is that significant?"

"I don't know. We'll see. It's visible from the road. If it was open, anyone passing would see it. And just over there . . ." I pointed past the double garage, at the backs of the houses that ran parallel along Powell Avenue. ". . . is where Sadie Byrne lived."

"Huh . . . pretty close. Almost visible from the top floor."

"Let's go get the keys."

We strolled down the street, among the mottled shade of the chestnut trees, listening to the raucous chatter of the starlings above in the green leaves, and the boisterous laughter of the kids in the playground opposite the houses. After we'd passed a few standalones, we came to a cute terrace of gabled redbricks, each with a flight of nine steps leading up to a porch set over a garage. The first was Mrs. Nowak's, and I climbed up to ring on the doorbell.

The door opened, and I had to look down to see her. She was four foot eleven and had hair the color of ripe tomatoes. A few strands of brown hair protruded from her upper lip, as though somebody had put them there by mistake. She studied my face with shrewd eyes, and then gave Dehan the same treatment.

"What?"

I showed her my badge. "NYPD. I'm Detective Stone; this is Detective Dehan. Are you Mrs. Nowak?"

"What if I yam?" Her voice was rapid and nasal.

"I believe Mrs. Inglewood has been in touch with you about the keys . . . ?"

"Don't come in! You not allowed to come in without a warrant! Stay there, on the stoop!"

She went away, into the shadows of the house, all knees and elbows and slippers. Desultory sounds: grunts, soft curses, and mild blasphemy wafted out to us, followed shortly by Mrs. Nowak holding a small key ring with a number of keys on it. She handed them to me, then yanked them back as I reached for them.

"You bring 'em back! They not mine, see! I ain't been in theya. I ain't touched nothin'! She gave 'em to me on trust. And I have to give 'em back to her when she sells the goddamn place. If she ever does!"

"We'll bring them right back."

"Cops, ain'tcha?" She slapped the keys in my hand, muttered something that sounded vile about "goddamn cops," and closed the door.

We made our way back down the steps. Dehan muttered, "And Angela Inglewood spent a couple of hours with that woman? Why would you do that?"

"Perhaps she was nicer back then."

She shook her head. "Uh-uh. It takes years to get like that. It's a process, like erosion, or developing a bunion."

We came to the Inglewoods' house. Dehan made for the front door, but I went 'round the side to have a look at the French windows. The drapes were drawn inside. I went and touched the doors, tried the handle. It felt solid. Dehan came 'round the corner to watch me, then joined me as I made my way to the rear of the house.

"Something's on your mind," she said. "I can tell."

"If it's not now," I said cryptically, "it will be soon."

She nodded. "Oh, should I hit you now, or wait till we get inside?"

"I'm just wondering how the killer got in."

We had got to the back of the house, and there was another door there. This one was a normal wooden door with a square pane of glass at the top that was reinforced with a kind of chicken-wire mesh inside it. It had two locks beneath an old-fashioned lever handle. One was Chubb, the other Yale. I pointed at the door.

"You reckon that door has a couple of dead bolts on the inside?"

"Yeah, I do, but you've clearly been thinking about this case for a while, Stone, and have formed some opinions already. Didn't you tell me the killer got in through the French windows?"

I nodded, stepping across the overgrown lawn to the far side of the house. "Yes. Well, what I in fact said was that Angela Inglewood said that she had gone to Mrs. Nowak's and left the French windows open."

She came after me, taking long strides. "So isn't that the obvious way in? Especially as it's visible from the road!"

I was surprised by the comment and showed her my surprise with my face. She grunted, "No, okay, you're right. Of course, seeing the door from the road and slipping in would suggest an opportunistic killing, and this killing was not in any way opportunistic. But still, I mean, if the doors were open . . ."

I nodded and made my way back to the front of the house, speaking over my shoulder. "That is important, very important."

I came to the front door, pulling out the key from my pocket. Dehan followed slowly, watching her feet. "So maybe he'd been watching, casing the joint, waiting for an opportunity."

"That's possible."

"Somebody with a grudge . . ."

"Definitely."

"Who had been watching and waiting, and when Angela went out, he saw the door open and seized the opportunity."

I unlocked the door, pushed, and stepped inside.

The first impression was the unpleasant, fetid smell on the air. The place was in shadow, with only occasional shafts of dusty light piercing the gloom. It took a moment for my eyes to adjust, and then I saw that we were stepping into a very large space that stretched out on either side of the front door. There was no fireplace, and the room had more the feel of a lounge in a hotel or an airport than a living room. There was a huge white leather sofa in the middle of the floor, with two vast, overstuffed white leather armchairs opposite, and in the middle a white wrought iron, glass, and brass coffee table. On one wall, to the left as we came in, there was a TV the size of a small cinema screen, with four independent speakers dotted about the room. So you could evade the real world and make the fake world seem as real as the one you were escaping from.

There was a flight of stairs at the back, rising in a dogleg to what I figured was an attic space above. A door beside the stairs led to the back of the house. I guessed there would be a kitchen and a bathroom. And over on the right, with the drapes drawn across them, were the French windows, which had stood open and admitted Chuck Inglewood's killer, eighteen months ago. Dehan spoke, pointing at the drapes, where the dusty light filtered in like a weak halo around the dark oblong.

"He came in there. He crossed the room to the stairs . . ."

"Wooden stairs."

"Is that important?"

"They creak."

"Oh, okay, yeah, obviously. So, he crossed to the wooden stairs, he climbed them to the bedroom . . ." She paused. "So he must have been quick. Real quick. As you say, Chuck would have heard him, so he had to get up there before Chuck reacted." She paused, staring up at the top of the steps. "And in the bedroom he attacked him and killed him." She stared at me. "He must have known the house, and he must have known what he was going to find here."

I nodded and sighed. "Yes, let's go upstairs."

She led the way, and they creaked.

TWO

The stairs, which were noisy, went up through a hole in the ceiling to a floor where it was even gloomier than down below, and the rancid smell was worse. The landing was horseshoe-shaped, carpeted wall-to-wall in cream, with a door on the left and another opposite on the right. Dehan paused on the last step, glanced at the door on the left, and said, "That's got to be a john."

I watched her step up, open the door, and lean in; dim light filtered out across her face and her hair. "No," she said. "It's not a john. It's an office."

I went and stood beside her. It was a long, oblong room with panoramic windows overlooking the backyard and, over the rooftops, Powell Avenue, where the Byrnes lived. On the far right there was a two-seater sofa, an armchair, and a coffee table, and, running the length of the room under the window, he had a long desk. There were files and papers, mostly orders and tax returns, invoices and bills. A bank of plug sockets had been screwed to the wall, just below the windowsill. I pointed at it.

"I wonder where the computer is."

"Maybe they took it to the lab."

I shook my head. "Nothing about that in the file. We should ask."

I stepped out of the office and crossed the landing to the door opposite. The foul smell grew stronger as I approached. I heard Dehan swear behind me and glanced over my shoulder as I took hold of the handle.

"I don't think this place has been cleaned since he was killed."

She had her hand over her nose and mouth and nodded. Her voice came out muffled. "She just closed up the house and walked away."

I pushed open the door. The stench made me back away, fighting down the reflex to retch. Dehan swore again, turned, and walked to the banisters. "*Puta chingada!* Holy . . . ! Sweet mother of Jesus!" She turned and stared at me. "They took the body, right?"

I nodded. "But they didn't take the sheets."

I pulled the handkerchief from my pocket and covered my nose and mouth, then pushed through the door again. There was a window opposite the door, and another over on the left, overlooking the drive. Both were shut and both had the drapes closed, with only hazy light filtering around the sides. The bed was large, probably six foot six square, and it was swarming with flies. The duvet was roughly in place, as though the bed had recently been made and then rumpled slightly. In the half-light, it looked like the bedding was dark brown, or even black, but then I noticed that the rug on which the bed was standing, which should have been cream, was also dark.

Dehan spoke through the crook of her arm, which was covering her nose and mouth.

"She just walked away . . . She left the bed, with all his blood . . ."

"That smell isn't the blood, Dehan, not after eighteen months."

She glanced at me over her arm. ". . . rats."

I looked around. On my left, across the polished wood floor, a door stood half-open onto a tiled en suite bathroom that was in deep shadows. I crossed the room, pulled back the drapes, and opened the window. Dehan did the same at the other end of the room. Air and bright sunlight streamed in and flooded the room and the bed. There was a flurry of rustles and scrabbling, and a rat darted from under the bed and scuttled into the en suite.

"We'll have to get pest control in here. Look..."

On the far side, away from the door, the carpet, the duvet, and parts of the mattress, where they had been saturated with blood, had been chewed, eaten away. Dehan hunkered down and peered under the bed. Her nose wrinkled and her nostrils dilated.

"There are holes in the wall. They've chewed right through, but there are..." She paused while she counted. "At least six dead rats here, and a couple of plastic trays."

She stood, pulled her cell from her pocket, and made the call. While she was doing that, I went into the bathroom. There was a tube of toothpaste on the sink, two toothbrushes in a glass. In the cabinet there was a bottle of painkillers, a couple of disposable razors, a box of tampons, floss. A tall cabinet against the wall, beside the bathtub, held towels and toilet rolls. Behind the shower curtain, at the end of the bath, I found shampoo, shower gel, a pink disposable razor.

When I returned to the bedroom, I found Dehan, with her hands on her hips, standing at the top of the stairs, staring down over the banisters.

"So what happened here, Stone?" She began to move down the stairs as she spoke. "It's early afternoon. We don't know where he is. Maybe he's in his office, working. Maybe he's in the kitchen, clearing up after lunch. Whatever..."

She had reached the bottom of the stairs and was looking around the living room. I stood beside her, trying to visualize the scene.

"She goes to him, or she calls to him, 'I'm going down the road to visit with Mrs. Nowak.'"

She pointed across the room to the drapes, then walked over

and pulled them back. The midday sun glared in. She held out her hands to me, and I tossed her the keys. She unlocked the glass doors and slid them back so that fresh, bright air entered the room.

"These doors are open," she said. "So, in all probability, she leaves through here, right? Or does she go to the front door? It doesn't matter, either way, she leaves. She goes out and down to the sidewalk, she turns right and walks for a minute or less, climbs the stairs to the stoop, and goes in to have coffee."

She stopped, and I took over. "And we assume that Chuck's killer, who is nearby, sees her do that. Meanwhile, wherever he is, and whatever he is doing, Chuck winds up going upstairs to the bedroom. What made him do that? If the bathroom is as they left it, like the rest of the house, there are no towels waiting to be washed, no clothes on the floor, no indication that he had just had a bath or a shower. Also, his body was dressed. So maybe he went up to work, but then why is he in the bedroom? What made him go to the bedroom?"

She was facing me, silhouetted against the bright sunlight. There was now a faint smell of sweet roses on the air.

"Okay, let's park that to one side for now. We know he wound up upstairs because that's where his body was found and that's where all his blood was. What made him go up there, we don't know, for now. But for the sake of the argument, let's say he was in his office; Angela had gone, so there is nobody downstairs. The killer sees her leave and sees the French doors are open. So he comes in. Here it gets tricky . . ."

I walked past her and stepped out onto the broad, concrete drive. The day was growing warm. I glanced over to the shade of the plane trees that fringed the road. Dehan was in the doorway behind me, leaning on the jamb. I said:

"Okay, backtrack a minute. On the face of it we have two options: one, that the killer was passing and happened to notice the door was open, so went in and killed Chuck. That presents a couple of problems."

She nodded. "The first is that, as we said, it makes the killing opportunistic, while the way he was killed, and the fact that nothing was stolen, suggests that the killing was motivated by rage, hatred, revenge, something of that sort."

"Yeah, and the other thing is that"—I shook my head—"Chuck was not a small guy. He was in his thirties and strong, but there is no indication that there was any kind of fight or struggle. Even if you allow that a random man was passing who had a random compulsion to kill, who happened to have a knife with him and happened to see the French windows open, *and* went in, not knowing who the hell was in there, why the hell didn't Chuck defend himself?"

She scratched her cheek and looked away at the road, like she was trying to see the random guy with a knife. "Yeah," she said. "Random killer or not, that's a problem that is going to keep coming up. For now let's say that we discard the random passerby, and we go with the second option. Somebody has some kind of grudge against Chuck. They have been watching him, even stalking him."

I took a couple of steps back toward her, nodding. "So he is already armed. He has chosen a knife rather than a gun."

"Yeah, because he wants to make it a silent kill, but also, it is more personal this way."

I frowned. "Mm-hm, it is very personal, and also, this keeps nagging at me, Dehan, the *location* of the wounds." I took her arm by the wrist and lifted it with my left hand, pointing at her armpit and the inside of her biceps as I did so. "Deep cuts into the basilic vein and the brachial artery, on both arms. And then—"

I dropped onto one knee and pushed her right leg slightly to one side, pointing with my right hand to her inside thigh. "He cuts deep into the inside thigh, into the femoral artery, the femoral vein, and the saphenous..."

"You having fun down there, Stone?"

I looked up at her and smiled. "Try to stay on task, Dehan." I got to my feet. "Again, in *both* legs. And while he's doing this,

Chuck is passive, not fighting back. This guy was either some kind of ninja, or Chuck was drugged."

Dehan was squinting at me and lowered her shades over her eyes against the bright sun. "They must have done a tox. What did it say?"

I shook my head. "Nothing. No drugs were found in his system."

She turned and stepped back into the house. I followed.

"Killer comes in," I said. "Does he meet Chuck down here? Do they talk? If they do, whatever they talk about leads them upstairs..."

"But *not*..." She turned to face me. "... as you would expect, to the office. It leads them to the bedroom."

I grunted. "Where the killer pulls a knife and, within a fraction of a second, incapacitates Chuck, throws him on the bed, and goes to work on his arteries. This is impossible. It's insane."

"But it gets better, Stone." She walked away from me, toward the stairs, with her hands on her hips, then turned and walked back, telling me how it got better.

"Because, with the killer on his way down the stairs, or right there, with him, Chuck then calls his wife, *six times*. And when she doesn't answer, he calls 911. Now, he has to be damn quick." She pointed up at the bedroom, like she wanted me to see what was going on up there in her mind. "Because he is bleeding out fast. So either the killer *was* a damn ninja, did his work super fast and left..."

"Or he was still there when Chuck was making the calls..."

"And that is really disturbing."

"It's disturbing and makes as little sense as the rest of it." I paused, searching my mind for images that made sense, trying to make movies in my mind of a sequence of events that was logical and coherent. "What would his purpose be?"

"To draw her home. So perhaps she was also a target."

"But she didn't come. She said she saw half a dozen missed calls. They were talking, and she didn't hear the phone."

"So time passes, the killer panics and runs, and that's when he calls 911, just before losing consciousness and dying."

"And just before his wife gets home."

"She and the killer must have just missed each other by seconds."

I grunted. "And he never came back." I sighed loudly and ran my fingers through my hair. "That doesn't make sense either. If she was part of the target, why did he wait for her to leave, and why didn't he come back? And that brings us to the final thing that is playing on my mind, Dehan."

"I know." She reached behind her neck and tied her long, black hair into a knot. It was a gesture that never failed to distract me. "I know," she said again. "At this point, the killer, having severed the main arteries and veins in Chuck's body, having saturated the whole bed and the carpet in blood, walks out without leaving a single bloody footprint, a single handprint, not a single drop of blood in the house except the blood in the bedroom."

I shrugged. "How'd he do that? He cuts Chuck to pieces in seconds, waits a couple of minutes or less while he makes his calls, then exits without leaving a trace. Even if we said that he went into the bathroom and showered, which is in itself insane, where are the footprints across the floor? Did he mop those up too? And how long did it take him? Because he has a few minutes tops for Chuck to make his calls and bleed out before Angela gets home. And in that time he showered, changed his clothes, put the damp towel in the laundry basket, mopped the floor . . . How did he do that?"

She was quiet for a long while. I wandered to the kitchen and stood in the doorway for a moment, looking out through the window at the backyard. Over my shoulder I heard Dehan say, "He has some serious skills."

I found myself nodding absently as my eyes traveled below and to the left of the sink. There was the washing machine. I could see the folded shapes of clothes within, dark with mold. She had washed clothes that day, and never bothered to take them out.

"What are you staring at?"

She rested her chin on my shoulder. I gestured at the washing machine, then went and opened the dishwasher. All the cutlery, plates, pots, and pans from their last meal together were there.

"She may as well have come back," said Dehan.

I stood and looked at her. "What do you mean?"

She met my eye. "He destroyed her life as completely as though he had stabbed her in the heart."

"Yeah."

I found the pantry, and inside it I found a roll of garden refuse sacks. I peeled one off, hunkered down, and pulled all the moldy clothes out of the washing machine. The stench of stale detergent was about as bad as the smell of dead rats upstairs. I sealed the bag and stood for a moment. Dehan was frowning at me.

"What are you thinking?"

"I don't know. But something is wrong." I pulled out my cell and called Joe at the lab.

"Stone, how you doing? What's on your mind?"

"You remember the Inglewood case, about two years ago?"

"Nope. Should I?"

"It was an odd case, guy stabbed to death in his house, deep cuts to the insides of his thighs and arms. I thought you might remember. Anyway, listen, I'm at the house. It hasn't been touched since the murder. The bloody sheets are still on the bed. There are things, Joe, that just don't make sense to me. At the time, as far as I can see, no thorough inspection was made of the en suite bathroom upstairs. I guess there didn't seem to be a need. But, I'd like you to send a team and just go over that bathroom with a fine-tooth comb. Look for everything from prints to traces of blood, especially in the bath, but on the walls, tiles, floor . . . everywhere."

"Sure, give me the address. I'll send a team over right away."

"Thanks, and Joe? For the sake of completeness, take the sheets too. See what you can get from them."

I gave him the address and hung up. Dehan shrugged at me.

"I get it, but you're wasting your time. He didn't have time. It's that simple."

I shrugged back. "Where is the blood?"

THREE

I handed the house keys, and the bag of moldy washing, over to Joe and his crew, then strolled down to Mrs. Nowak to explain that we would be hanging on to the keys. She scowled at us through the half-open door and snarled, "I never went in there, see? I never put pawee-son down neither. That ain't my place to do that. Though there was rats enough to do it! God only knows!"

We assured her it had never crossed our minds, and we left her peering darkly through the crack in her door as we returned to the car. When we got there, I leaned on the roof and felt the heat seep through my jacket and into my arms. It was somehow reassuring. Dehan stood across from me.

"What now, big guy?"

"Now?" I looked up at the dappled green leaves of the chestnuts. "Now I could use a beer to wash away the smell of those rats. But first I think we go and talk to Angela Inglewood. Then we'll have some lunch and mull this over." I opened the door and stopped halfway in. "There is something very wrong with this, Dehan. Something's very wrong, and it ain't right."

We climbed in and slammed the doors, the cat growled, and we pulled away toward the Cross Bronx Expressway. It was a short drive, and at Pennyfield Avenue we took the exit and went down as far as Chaffee Avenue, a short cul-de-sac overlooking the Locust Point Marina. Angela Inglewood's house was one but last from the end, on the left.

It was a massive, double-fronted redbrick affair that looked mock-Georgian, with a Palladian, stucco portico and gabled dormers jutting out of the attic. A hedged path traversed the front lawn to six steps that ascended to the front door. I glanced at Dehan and, in silence, we made our way through the front yard.

Angela Inglewood opened the door almost immediately. She was a tall woman, almost six foot, slim and boney, with very white skin and very black hair pulled back into a severe bun at the base of her skull. Her eyes were a deep blue, and though they spoke of sympathy and kindness, her lips were tight and thin and told of a compassion that had withered into caution through lack of reciprocity from a world that didn't care.

She said, "You must be the detectives," like that was exactly the kind of thing she would expect from us.

We showed her our badges. "I am John Stone; this is my partner, Detective Dehan."

"You'd better come in."

She stood back, and we went into an old-fashioned hall where a mahogany staircase climbed to upper floors over a large, Spanish credenza, and heavy wooden doors opened to left and right into rooms you just knew she called parlors, where there were doilies on the chairs, coasters on the occasional tables, and the furniture had "do not disturb" signs on it.

She gestured us to the door on my right, and we followed her through it into a cozy room overcrowded with furniture that was pretending to be antique. The bookshelves had little room for books, because the space was taken up with small statues of kittens and milkmaids, and one of a humorously drunk Irishman leaning against a lamppost. You could tell he was Irish by his green hat.

She sat on the sofa, with her back to the window, and we each took an armchair. I drew breath to speak, trying to organize my thoughts, but she spoke first.

"You have seen the house now. I honestly don't know what you can hope to have found that the initial investigation missed." She shook her head. "I don't know what you hope I can tell you."

I let out the breath I'd drawn in as a small sigh.

"*I* don't honestly know, Mrs. Inglewood. But there are a few things that don't make a lot of sense to us at the moment."

She gave a laugh that was on the bitter side of harsh. "Sense? Does *any* of it make sense? A man is murdered in his own home, in broad daylight, in the middle of the afternoon! Nothing is stolen, nothing is taken, there is no apparent reason for the killing, and you are looking for sense?"

Dehan leaned forward with her elbows on her knees and her hands clasped.

"Mrs. Inglewood, my partner and I have been working homicide for many years. Between us we have racked up about thirty-five years of experience. You can imagine how many murders we have seen in that time."

Angela Inglewood looked momentarily chastened and averted her eyes. "A good few, I should imagine," she said.

Dehan nodded. "Yeah, a good few. A few of them, mainly those that are gang related, make a kind of sordid, brutal sense to the killers and to the victims, the pursuit of power or money. But the vast majority make no sense at all to anyone in their right minds. They make sense to the killer, and they have a twisted logic to people like my partner and me, who have learned over the years to understand the way these people's minds work. We don't think of it in terms of sense, or logic or sanity. We think in terms of motive."

Angela stared at her for a while, then her eyes shifted to me. I said, "We can't find anything that remotely suggests a motive in this case. But more than that, there are a number of facts that don't seem to fit into any kind of explanation for what happened. I am not going to trouble you with them now—I know how distressing it must be for you to have all this dragged up again—but I am going to ask you to try and think back. Was there anybody, anybody at all, who might have wished your husband harm? Who might have wanted to hurt him?"

Her expression was one of helplessness, shaking her head. "No! No, not at all. I won't say that everybody loved Chuck. They didn't. But nobody hated him either. Nobody even disliked him. He was a normal man. He worked hard, he had a bit of a temper, but he was . . ." She shrugged and spread her hands. It was a gesture of resignation. "He was just *unremarkable*. I guess that would be the word. That's why it's so senseless. I loved him because he was a hardworking man who cared deeply about his family. We couldn't have kids. We found that out early on. But he did everything he could for us."

"What about in business? Did he ever cross anyone, make an enemy, borrow from a loan shark . . . ?"

For a moment her face lit up with amusement, and for a second it was a nice face, pretty and humorous. She laughed. "Chuck? No! He never borrowed. 'You don't pay money for money,' he used to say. And as for making enemies, that wasn't the way he *did* business. He did business by cultivating loyal friends. If he did business with you, he made damn sure you were happy. But if he didn't get his pound of flesh, if he wasn't happy with you, he never did business with you again. That was the end of it." She trailed off, gazing down at her hands neatly laid in her lap. "So to answer your questions, no. He had no enemies. He didn't have great friends—there wasn't a huge turnout at his funeral—but nobody hated Chuck. Not many people really loved him either, but those who knew him well respected him."

We were silent for a while, Angela looking down at her hands, Dehan watching her. I sighed, and it sounded loud in that gloomy room.

"Mrs. Inglewood, I am sorry, but I have to ask you this." She looked up to meet my gaze, and her eyes were startlingly blue and intense. "Was there another man?"

She immediately sat up straight, squaring her shoulders. I held up my hands, placating. She said, "How dare you!"

"I don't mean at the same time..."

Dehan stepped in. "What Detective Stone means is, was there ever, at any time, another man?"

"Certainly not!"

"Mrs. Inglewood," Dehan persisted. "Think before you answer. You are an attractive woman." Angela looked startled. Dehan ignored her. "Is it possible: an old boyfriend, a suitor, even someone you turned away...?"

Angela shook her head, but there was something uncertain in the gesture. Something about the way she knit her brow suggested the question confused her, like the thought had never occurred to her before.

"No... Men have never..." She left the statement unfinished and instead said, "Chuck was the only man in my life. There was never anybody else."

"You see..." I hesitated, and she watched me. Her eyes said she didn't like my questions, and she didn't like me any better. Dehan stepped in again.

"Mrs. Inglewood, we think that the original investigation may have foundered partly because they missed a key point."

Angela's blue eyes shifted back to Dehan. "What point?"

"That your husband was not the sole, intended victim."

"*What?*"

"We think, for reasons we really don't want to go into right now, that you were intended to return while the killer was there."

Her skin, already pale, turned ghostly. "The phone calls."

Dehan nodded. "Yes, the phone calls. We think they were intended to lure you home. Which would suggest that your husband's death might have been intended in some way as a punishment for you."

Her voice was barely a whisper. "That's insane."

I spoke quietly. "I don't want to go into the details, but whichever way you look at it, there is no escaping the fact that the killer's behavior is hard to explain unless he intended you to be there."

Her eyes went wide. "Why?"

"Because he must have been there while your husband was trying to call you. He must have watched him do it, and allowed it. And that must mean, perforce, that in some way, somehow, you have some kind of connection or relationship with the killer, even if you are not immediately aware of it."

"That's . . ." She trailed off. "That's not possible. No. I can't believe that."

"You need to think, Mrs. Inglewood. Don't try to answer it now, but think about it."

She stood and clasped her hands in front of her, like two hooks linked across her belly. She walked to the window but didn't look out at the silent trees in the afternoon. She stared instead, unseeing, down at the windowsill. I gave her a while and then spoke.

"There is something else, Mrs. Inglewood."

"Something else? This isn't enough?"

"What kind of relationship did you and your husband have with your niece, Sadie?"

She screwed up her brow hard at the windowsill before turning to look at me.

"Sadie?" I waited. Dehan watched her, curious. "Relationship? She was our niece. She lived across the way. What kind of relationship . . . ?" She shrugged. "I don't know what you're getting at?"

"Were you fond of her? Did she visit often?"

She turned toward us now, with her back to the bright glass. Her face was cast in deep shadow so her expression was invisible.

"Of course. She was our niece. My sister lived on the next street. We visited often, and they visited us. Why are you asking about Sadie?"

"Sadie was raped."

"Yes. I know."

"A few months before your husband was murdered."

"Almost a year before."

"It is a big coincidence."

"You can't possibly think . . ." She couldn't say the words, so she said, "What are you suggesting?"

Dehan answered. "We're not suggesting anything, Mrs. Inglewood. But we have to wonder whether the two incidents aren't connected. Whatever the truth may be, is it possible that somebody got it into their head that your husband raped Sadie? After all, she refused to name her rapist, or even say where and when it had happened. Could this have been revenge?"

She stared around the floor, searching, as though she might find that absurd person there and give them the sharp end of her tongue. "Who?" she said. "Who could think that?"

I said, "We're not suggesting it, Mrs. Inglewood. We are just asking if it is possible. A boyfriend, even your brother-in-law . . ."

"No!" She shook her head violently, not looking at us. "No, no, no! What you are suggesting is insane! You are . . ." She faltered, searching for a word strong enough. ". . . *completely* wrong, on the wrong track, wrong! Patrick is a good, kind man. Sadie was a normal teenager. Her friends were just normal kids. This *thing* you are suggesting is just *wrong*!"

"Okay." I stood. "Mrs. Inglewood, we are very sorry to have distressed you. All we want is to find who did this to Chuck."

At the sound of his name she froze and stared up into my face. I went on.

"Whoever did it is a very sick person, who may have wanted to harm you too, so we are going to leave no stone unturned searching for them." I smiled at her, spoke quietly. "If you'll forgive me for taxing the metaphor, turning some of those stones has to be painful. But we have to do it. It is one hell of a coincidence, that both of these things should happen within a few months of each other." I nodded. "And it may be just that, a coincidence. But it also may be that somebody, for some reason, believed that Chuck had raped Sadie. And we have to explore that possibility. So you need to think about that. You need to think about who, in your circle of family, friends, and wider acquaintances, might have had a grudge against Chuck. Possibly somebody who was close to Sadie. Can you do that for us?"

She had become more calm as I spoke to her. Now she nodded, once, slowly, then a couple of times more quickly, as though she had come to some decision.

"Yes, I'll do that. I'm sorry. It is all so fresh. He was my rock, my pillar. He took care of me, of everything. And . . ."

She shook her head, then seemed to crumple onto the sofa. Her pretty, white face became pink and distorted, shiny with a sudden discharge of tears. Dehan sat next to her and put her arms around her. She tried to talk, but all that came out were distorted, twisted sounds, until she buried her face in Dehan's shoulder and clung to her.

I sat.

After a few minutes her convulsive crying stopped, her breathing steadied, and she pulled away from Dehan. I handed her a handkerchief, which she took, blew her nose, and dabbed her eyes.

"I'm sorry," she said again. "I still have trouble accepting that he's gone."

"I'm so sorry we have to . . ." I shrugged and spread my hands.

She shook her head. "It has to be done. I'll do my best to think about what you've said. I'll talk to Cathy. I'll see if anything occurs to me."

We thanked her, and she showed us out.

Midday had matured into a golden afternoon as we made our way between the hedges to the sidewalk where the Jaguar was parked. Dehan leaned with the heels of her hands on the roof and shook her head, looking at me through dark shades. "Man!" she said. "It doesn't get easier."

"Nope. Pepperoni pizza and beer might take the edge off, though."

"The man has wisdom."

We climbed in, and I sat awhile with the key in my hand, staring at the fringe of trees that marked the end of the cul-de-sac, where the banks ran down to the creek. I didn't see them though. All I could see was the open French windows on the Inglewoods' drive, and a figure stepping in, from the sunlight to the shadows within. An anonymous figure, almost shapeless, who moved silently through the house, up the stairs, and confronted Chuck Inglewood with a very sharp knife.

And cut him. Cut him deeply and cruelly, and left him to bleed to death. And not a drop of that blood stained the killer.

"Stone?"

I turned and looked at Dehan. She had raised her shades on top of her head, like a knight's visor, and she was frowning and smiling at me. I smiled back. "What?"

"Come back. It's lunchtime."

"*Andiamo!*" I said, facetiously, and turned the key in the ignition. "*Andiamo a mangiare la pizza!*"

"Yeah," she said. "What the man said." And we pulled away.

FOUR

We ended up going to Tosca Rooftop Bar and having hamburgers with mature cheddar cheese, instead of a pizza. The important thing was that the beer was cold, and welcome. Dehan sat with her elbows on the table and her sleeves rolled up, with the burger held in both hands, chewing, watching me. She let go with her right hand so she could stab her finger in my direction.

"What if," she said, and swallowed. "What if Sadie was never raped?"

I leaned back and thought about it while I chewed back at her. I shook my head and took a pull on my beer. "It makes no difference."

"How so?" She took another bite.

"Because all that's necessary is that somebody *believed* she was raped, and decided to punish the Inglewoods."

She waved her finger and maneuvered her words around a mouthful of beef and cheese. "But suppose she was not raped, she was just seeking attention, it happens. Suppose further that it was her uncle's attention she was after, and she was punishing him for ignoring her. It happens, an adolescent crush."

"What are you saying, that she set somebody up to do it and it went wrong?"

"I don't know. What troubles me is, it looks like it was directed at both of them. If the motive was the rape, Angela would not be an intended victim . . ."

I interrupted, "I know. And if she was an intended victim, you have to wonder why the killer never came back. That troubles me too."

"He stalks Chuck, seizes his chance, takes a huge risk just so he can punish her as well, then runs off and never comes back. Why? Hell, he was so damned ineffectual she doesn't even know he exists! Some punishment!"

I sighed and bit into my own burger. "Maybe he scared himself half to death with what he did and couldn't see it through."

"Maybe."

"Or maybe we're seeing it all wrong."

"That's a maybe too. What if the murder was not a punishment for the rape, but the rape was part of the punishment."

I raised an eyebrow. "Interesting, punishment for what?"

She shrugged and pulled off half her beer. "I don't know. It's just a random thought under the heading, 'There are no bad ideas in brainstorming.' But it might explain why he never came back."

I shook my head. "I'm not following you."

She stuffed the last piece of burger in her mouth and wiped ketchup from her fingers while she chewed.

"He had AIDS. He became ill, went into the hospital, died . . ."

I made a face that was skeptical. "With antiretroviral drugs most people with HIV lead perfectly normal lives."

"Most people, people who seek treatment, people who take their medication. But what about a junkie?"

"That's reaching, Dehan. We don't know she had any junkie friends."

"That's true, but it could explain the bizarre nature of the killing. Sustained use of any kind of drugs can lead to psychotic episodes. I'm just spitballing here, Stone. But we haven't much to go on save the damned weird nature of the murder, and the rape. Now, if they are connected, maybe they are connected the other way around from what we assumed."

I stuffed the last bit of my burger in my mouth, echoing her and wiping my fingers on a paper napkin.

"Explain, I'm not following you."

"Angela said this guy was devoted to his family, right? They couldn't have kids, so maybe they were a bit more devoted to the niece, lived 'round the corner, almost like a Latin family. And maybe he was protective . . ." She shrugged and pulled down the corners of her mouth and made it look Italian. "Maybe there was an incident, this is the Bronx, some kid said something, did something, and he stepped in to defend her or protect her . . . who knows. Maybe we should find out."

"Eh, Dino, donna messa with de family, ah?"

"Right. So Dino, or Chavez or O'Conor, whatever his name is, punishes her by raping her, and then goes to visit the protective uncle. Retribution, Bronx style." She picked some sesame seeds from her plate. "Inglewood, what is that, German, English?"

"I don't know. Sadie was Byrne, that's Irish. And Angela was Ryan before she married. Irish too."

She shrugged again. "You don't need to be Catholic or Jewish to protect your family."

"It's a hell of a reach. But all we have right now are theories, so maybe we should look into that angle. God knows we have little enough to go on. So we need to talk to Cathy and Patrick Byrne, Sadie's parents, find out who her friends were and if there were any incidents of the type you're suggesting. Also ask Cathy if Angela had any previous boyfriends, suitors, lovers . . . I don't buy her line that Chuck was the only man in her life."

"Neither do I. You want a coffee?" I nodded, and she leaned back in her chair making the peace sign at the waiter. "Eh!" she said, loudly and obnoxiously, "*Gino! Due espressi! Sbrigati!*"

He rolled his eyes and went to make the coffee while Dehan grinned at me and said, "What?" She drained her beer, set down the glass, and smacked her lips. "The Italians and the Jews have a very complex relationship, Stone. Did you know that?"

"No, but I fear you are going to explain it to me."

"Yeah. Basically, they wish they were us. We both have this big, noisy, Mediterranean family thing going on. But they, because of the Romans, the Vatican, and the legacy of the empire, all that stuff, they wanted to have the whole 'world control through banks and Bilderberg conspiracy' thing too. You know we control the world through Hollywood and the banks, right?" I gave a weary nod. "But the best they could do was the Mafia, and now the Mexicans, the Albanians, and the Russians have beat them at that too. So they wish they were us."

"You have a troubled mind, Dehan. You know we'll have the thought police knocking on our door one of these days if you keep that up."

"Thought police schmought police! We *own* the thought police! Adam Weishaupt, a Jewish Mason and founder of the Illuminati, created the thought police in 1777, after he escaped from Bavaria, murdered George Washington, and replaced him as his double."

"You're a strange woman, Dehan. You know that?"

The waiter brought our coffee and left. Dehan flapped a hand at me.

"Yeah, yeah, yadda yadda." She sipped. "I was just thinking about my dad. He used to defend me and Mom. He didn't realize I was always trying to defend him and Mom too. He stood up to the Chupacabras and an Irish cop, as you well know, and it cost him his life. Family. Is it family, in the end? Power? Control?"

"Well, speaking of thought police, Orwell said that what everyone was after in the end was power. But I am not sure that it applies to this case. I think your dad was probably just a good guy."

She drained her cup. "You don't think it applies in this case?

Are you sure? Rape, after all, Stone, is not really a sexual crime, though it may feel that way to the victim. It is all about power, isn't it. The attacker seeks to dominate and control the victim, and subjugate them. Thinking about it, if you kill somebody by cutting their arteries and letting them bleed out, while they call for help on their cell phone, you're doing pretty much the same thing: disempowering them and controlling them."

I nodded several times, with my coffee cup halfway to my mouth.

"That is very insightful, Dehan." I drained my cup too and called for the check, then added, "Of course, if I had made that observation, you would have said something like . . ."

"What? Are you a psychiatrist now?"

"Yeah, something like that."

She laughed and stood. "Yeah, well, it's power, see? I grew up on the mean streets, Stone—I know all about power."

I stood too and propelled her toward the door. "Quit while you're ahead, kiddo. Quit while you're ahead."

Dehan planted her ass against the trunk of the car and called Cathy Byrne. Cathy told her she was at home, but her husband was still at work. Dehan said we'd drop by anyway.

It was a short drive, via the Bruckner Interchange and Castle Hill, to Powell Avenue. Number 1984 was a cute, detached redbrick complete with a white picket fence, a white, wrought iron porch, and a tall chimney pot over a sharp gabled roof. It looked like a house where nice, happy people lived. I climbed the five stone steps to the white door and rang the bell.

Cathy Byrne was like the beta version of her older sister. She had the same black hair, but it was tied in a loose ponytail instead of a bun. Her eyes were the same startling, deep blue, though the fear they showed was untamed and undisciplined, and her mouth still knew how to smile. Her skin, too, was very white. Though I wondered how much of that was due to our visit.

We showed her our badges and introduced ourselves. She

stood back to let us in, apologizing as she did so. She apologized with the easy fluidity of a person who has made a habit of it.

"I'm afraid Patrick is at work. He lectures at the college, you know. English literature. Otherwise he would have been here. I'm not sure . . ." She trailed off.

We were in an entrance area that was enclosed only by two sets of banisters that served no real purpose, except to tell you you were not yet inside the room "proper." There was a coat stand, an umbrella stand, and a bowl full of keys. And beyond these there was a parquet floor that stretched into a living space, comfortably furnished with large, soft, dark brown leather armchairs and a suede sofa that did not match, but worked. They were set rather carelessly around a large fireplace. There was no coffee table, but lamp tables and occasional tables were set strategically so that each chair, and each end of the sofa, was catered to. Bookcases, occupied by well-thumbed books and a few ornaments, lined the available wall space. At the far end of the room there was a large, heavy dining table and an open kitchen.

Cathy did not finish her sentence. Instead she gestured with an open hand toward the sofa and the chairs.

"I'm sorry, will you have some coffee?"

Dehan sat. I said, "No, thanks, Mrs. Byrne."

"Cathy, please." She smiled nervously, asking for approval. "We don't stand on ceremony in this house."

I smiled like I understood. "We won't take much of your time. We just have a few questions."

I sat in a chair. She perched on the edge of the sofa and at right angles to me.

"Don't think me rude," she said. "But I'm really not sure what it is you want. After Sadie passed, they told us—the investigating detective told us there was nothing more they could do because there was no forensic evidence and, now that she was gone, there were no witnesses."

I made a "well, kinda" face. "That is true to some extent, Mrs. . . ." I smiled. "Cathy, but we are approaching the case from a new angle. We are actually investigating the murder of your brother-in-law."

Her eyes and her mouth formed three perfect Os. "Really? But what . . . ?"

"We are wondering whether the two are connected."

"*Connected?* How?"

Dehan gave a small snort. "Well, that's what we're trying to work out. It looks like a duck and it walks like a duck. But we can't quite work out which end is the beak and which end lays the eggs." Cathy Byrne looked slightly bewildered by the metaphor. I knew how she felt. Dehan went on regardless. "I mean, was there anyone hanging around that might have had a grudge? An ex-employee Chuck had fired, an old flame of Angela's, an old suitor, maybe some guy Sadie had jilted . . ."

Cathy laughed, clenching her fists and her elbows close to her body. "Oh, heavens, no!"

Dehan smiled. "Right. I mean, no to what exactly?"

"I'm sorry. I can be a bit vague. Patrick is always telling me so."

"Angela never had any lovers, boyfriends . . . I'm sorry to be blunt."

"Good Lord, no!"

"How about Sadie?"

Cathy seemed to zone out at the question, so I stepped in, seeming to change the subject. "How close was Sadie to her uncle, Cathy?"

Cathy smiled. "Oh, they were very close. He was a good man. Very devoted, very family oriented. They couldn't have children, you know? That was established long ago. So Sadie was a kind of surrogate. She used to go and visit, especially when she was younger, and they'd spoil her and fuss over her. She loved it, of course." She leaned forward confidentially, even though her husband was not in the house, and mouthed elaborately, "Patrick isn't much of a father figure, you know, but Chuck was more, sort of *manly*."

"Sure, more manly. So, Cathy, I hate to ask this, but was there anyone among Chuck and Angela's friends, or even Sadie's, that you were ever uncomfortable about? Who maybe you thought you'd prefer Sadie didn't hang out with?"

Her face clouded over and she frowned. "Well, not . . ."

I interrupted before she finished her answer. "Or who, perhaps, Chuck didn't like or disapproved of? You said he was very protective."

She hesitated some more. "Oh, well, not really among their friends. But there was somebody, I mean, I don't want to get anybody into trouble."

I smiled with my face but left my eyes and my voice out of it. "We deal in facts, Cathy. Nobody will get into trouble unless they've done something wrong."

"Yes, of course, I didn't mean. I'm sorry. Of course. I shouldn't have said that. Well, there was a boy Sadie used to hang out with, um . . ." Her eyes glazed as she tried to recall the name. "Gore, that wasn't his real name. Um . . . I don't know what his real name was. They just called him Gore. A nickname. I always thought he was harmless, boisterous, a bit noisy, but basically a good boy. But Chuck didn't like him at all. I used to tell Angela, if Gore's here, don't bring Chuck. He'll just make a scene."

"What kind of scene?"

She laughed. "Oh, well, Gore was a bit provocative. He especially liked to provoke Chuck and Angela, always talking about anarchy and freedom from parental authority. He had a mouth on him, I can tell you! Patrick couldn't stand him either. He would leave the room if Gore was here. But Chuck was more obstinate. He'd say, 'Why should I leave my own sister-in-law's living room just because some bigmouth has no manners?' And I suppose he had a point."

Dehan said, "So Chuck would call him out?"

"Yes, 'Watch your mouth in front of the ladies!' kind of thing."

"How did Sadie feel about that?"

"It annoyed her." She laughed a shrill laugh. "In fact it made her crazy! If Gore was here and she thought Chuck was coming, she'd leave."

"So was there ever an actual incident . . . ?"

Cathy looked doubtful. "Well, I suppose, I mean . . . I wouldn't want to make too much of it, but there was this one time."

I said, "What happened, Cathy?"

She sighed. "I *really* don't want you to go drawing conclusions from this."

Dehan leaned in close. "You'd better tell us. Your brother-in-law was murdered, Cathy. This is serious."

"Well, it's just, Gore was like a great big puppy. He could be annoying, but there was no malice in him. He just had no sense of what was *appropriate*. So he would bounce around, knock things over, say things he shouldn't, he was noisy and, well, he and Sadie were very close. So he used to hug her a lot, maybe a bit too tight in a way that was, well, a bit much. But she didn't mind, and she used to hug him back. Sometimes he'd even hug *me*! Well, *I* didn't mind and Patrick, frankly, thought it was funny to see Chuck getting so hot and bothered."

"But Chuck didn't like it, so what happened?"

"It was a Sunday in December, about a week before Christmas. Angela and I had been out, Christmas shopping, and Pat and Chuck had offered to make the Sunday lunch. Well, we'd only just got in, Pat was roasting a couple of chickens, Chuck was setting the table, and, well, Sadie turns up with Gore."

Dehan frowned. "So, was Gore, like, her boyfriend?"

"No! Oh no, just a friend. But she'd told us she was going to be out all Sunday, you see? So there was not enough food for them. Me and Pat, we said two chickens between six was okay, but Chuck was annoyed. He told Sadie she should have let us know. That she took her family for granted and she should be more respectful. So Gore told him if he didn't like it why didn't he go home, then there'd be enough food. And anyway, it was Sadie's house, not his. Well, you can imagine, Chuck didn't like that at all. He told Gore that his problem was nobody had ever taught him manners." She threw her hands in the air. "Well! After that it just got crazy. Gore started using foul language. Chuck yelled at Sadie, telling her she shouldn't hang out with losers like Gore..."

She stopped suddenly, staring at Dehan. I was about to ask her if that was it, when she said, "And that was when it happened."

Dehan asked, "What happened?"

"Gore went hysterical. He screamed at Chuck. 'You don't like me hanging out with your mh-mh'—he used the *F* word—'niece? Well let me tell you, you...'" She went bright red. "'... mother effer, I'll *F* her whenever I like and there's *F* all you can do about it!' And then he sort of jumped on her and grabbed hold of her and started kissing her, and sort of thrusting himself into her, even though she was trying to push him off and telling him to stop."

She paused. We said nothing. After a moment she said, "Well, Patrick and I were shaken, obviously. We're not naïve, but that was a bit shocking. But *Chuck*, he was furious. He was out of his mind! He went and grabbed Gore by the collar and sort of punched him." She made a jab with her fist to illustrate the punch. "He punched him in the back. I didn't think it would hurt, but it seemed to. Then he grabbed him by the hair and started hitting him again and again in the same place. Poor Gore was falling, kind of buckling at the knees, but Chuck wouldn't let him go. Then he turned him around and gave him a terrific punch in the face. Gore just fell down. Sadie was screaming. Angela and Patrick and I were just frozen. We didn't know what to do. Chuck sort of dragged Gore to his feet and screamed into his face, 'Don't you ever go near my niece again!' and he threw him out of the house."

We sat in silence for a while. Dehan was biting her lip. After a moment she said, "Cathy, did it never occur to you that this might be relevant to Chuck's murder investigation?"

Cathy looked genuinely bewildered. "No. Surely you don't think that Gore would have killed Chuck. That's ridiculous. Why, he's just a big puppy."

Dehan closed her eyes and shook her head. "What happened after that, Cathy?"

"Not much, it was very embarrassing. Chuck came back in, shaking with anger. He was all red, and he lectured me and Pat on how badly we had brought Sadie up. He said we were too lax and too liberal, and if we didn't change our ways we'd come to regret it. Halfway through Sadie ran upstairs to her room, crying."

She seemed to sag, and an expression of infinite sadness came over her. "I have to say, sometimes now I think back to what he said and I wonder if he hadn't been right, after all. It was just shortly after that, that Sadie was raped, and a few months after that she was dead."

I nodded. "And so was Chuck." She looked at me like she was shocked, like she hadn't known that before. I felt a sudden irritation at her stupidity, which I fought to suppress. "What happened to Gore after that? Did you ever see him again? Did Sadie?"

"He never came here again." She gave her head a little shake. "We used to ask after him, especially Patrick, encouraged her to bring him home sometimes, even though Gore got on Patrick's nerves. We felt sorry for him, and a bit responsible. But she never did, though I think she still saw him sometimes."

"You know where we can find him?"

She seemed to sag and collapse and made a crying face. "Oh *please*, you're not going to arrest him or hurt him, are you? I'm *sure* he's not . . ."

"*Mrs. Byrne!*" She came up short, startled by my tone. "Withholding evidence in a homicide investigation is a very serious offense! Two people are dead! One of them is your *daughter*! And this man may be responsible! Now will you please tell us where we can find him!"

She swallowed hard. "I don't know. Maybe in Sadie's cell phone. Or Ad or Poppy might know."

"Ad, Poppy?"

"Adriel, he was her sort of boyfriend, though they don't really do that these days, do they? They just hang. And Poppy was her best friend."

"Again, on her cell?"

"I believe you still have her things. We never got them back, and we didn't like to ask, in case . . ." She stood in a hurry. "But I have Ad's cell number. I can give you that."

She went to her own cell on the sideboard, looked through it, and made a note with a pen on a piece of paper, which she handed to me. I thanked her and we stood. She led us to the door, and there I turned and faced her, and took hold of her shoulder.

"Cathy, forgive me for being blunt, but you need to wake up and smell the coffee. Your daughter may well have been maliciously infected with HIV, and there is no maybe about the fact that your brother-in-law was murdered in the most cruel and sadistic way. The person who did this knew them both well, and the chances are very high that you know the person who did it. You may even know them well. If you think of anything, however trivial, that might be relevant, do *not* dismiss it. Contact us immediately."

I handed her a card and we left.

FIVE

Dehan punched me in the shoulder as I slipped the key in the ignition.

"So, who's a clever girl, huh? Huh? Huh? Tell me, did I call it right or, on the other hand, conversely, did I call it right? Wait, let me answer this one. Oh, I got it! I called it *right*! Huh? *Huh?*"

Each "Huh?" was accompanied by a well-delivered right jab.

"It was an inspired call, Dehan. No question about it."

"So where to now, boss? Whaddawedo now?"

I didn't answer until we had turned onto White Plains Road, headed south.

"I want to look at Sadie's phone and her social media. I want to see who she hung out with, who she talked to, all that stuff . . . see if we can track down this Gore and her other pals."

"They should all be in Evidence. There must be printouts."

"Probably. I also want to talk to Frank about Chuck's injuries." I shook my head. "I still don't get how that happened. I just can't visualize it."

"It's weird all right." She leaned her elbow on the open window and stared out at the passing clapboard houses in pastel blues and yellows as we cruised past. "What makes a guy just lie there and let somebody do that to him? It's nuts. And the injuries, Stone, they are all on the *inside*. Inside arms, inside thighs. It's weird."

"There is absolutely no indication that he struggled, or fought back..."

"He must have. He had to. I mean, the pain alone, Stone. It must have hurt like hell!"

I sighed and shook my head again. "I need to understand how that happened. That, right there, is the key. We understand that and we understand everything else."

She stared at me a moment, then nodded and turned away. "I agree. Then we need to track down those kids. I'd like to get my hands on that Gore for fifteen minutes. If you ask me, Chuck did him a favor. It's a shame more kids don't have dads like Chuck."

I smiled at her but said nothing. After a while she added, "We didn't talk to Cathy about the rape."

I frowned. "What do you mean?"

"I mean, we mentioned it, but we didn't ask her about how they found out, what Sadie said..."

I grunted and made a face. She was right. "I wanted to focus on Chuck, and her relationships. When Dad is available we can talk to them both about the rape. Something tells me he is probably a more observant witness. Something in particular you wanted to ask her?"

"I don't know. Maybe. I'm still kind of wondering if she was ever raped at all."

I was surprised, and my face told her so. "Yeah, you said that before."

"I don't know, Stone. I just get a feeling. You know." She slapped my shoulder with the backs of her fingers. "Liberal parents, academics, permissive upbringing, kid's allowed to do what the hell she likes, hangs out with freaks like Gore... Kids like that, often as not what they're really looking for from their parents is care and attention. It's a real fine line between 'be free' and 'get out of my hair.' But the parents are so caught up in their liberal, permissive ego trips: 'Oh look at me, I am so free and easy-going!' they don't realize the kid just wants a proper mom or dad to give a damn, guide her, get mad at her if she's naughty!"

She waved a finger at me. "It would not be the first time, Stone, that a middle-class kid, from a liberal, permissive background, came home telling her parents she's been raped, just because she wanted them to *care* that she'd come home at four a.m.!" She spread her hands. "Why did she wait so long to tell them? Why did she refuse to tell them who did it, and where?"

"That's not unusual either, Dehan. It's a very traumatic experience for a young woman, especially if the rapist was somebody she knew."

"Yeah. So is being mugged, or hit by a car, or having your house burgled. But people report that sh . . . stuff. Another reason for not reporting it is because it never happened, and she doesn't want her friends to get pulled in as suspects by the cops. But she *does* want Mommy and Daddy to fuss over her."

"That's pretty harsh, Dehan."

"So's life, Stone."

I was quiet for a bit. We crossed over the expressway, and I turned right into Story Avenue.

"So, if she wasn't raped, how did she get AIDS?" But I knew the answer before I'd finished asking the question. She snorted and shrugged. "The way most people get it. She slept around and she didn't use a condom. I'm telling you, Stone. I've got this kid's number."

I parked opposite the station house and killed the engine.

"So if you're right, and right now there is no way of knowing if you are or not, but if you are, how does this affect our investigation?"

She opened her door and stuck one long leg out. "It simplifies it, big guy. She caught HIV from one of her friends, who probably got it from using a dirty needle. It may even have been Gore. Chuck gave Gore a hiding to teach him some manners. Gore got sore and started to harbor hatred toward Chuck. When Sadie died it pushed him over the edge and he spilled over into psychosis. He went and killed Chuck, probably . . ." She nodded several times, pointing at me. ". . . probably projecting his own damned guilt onto Chuck, and then went and died somewhere in a gutter, which was why he never followed up."

"You are one harsh baby, Dehan."

"Life is harsh, Stone. I am merely a realist."

She finished climbing out, and I followed her across the road and into the building.

We spent half an hour in the evidence vaults and came up with a couple of cartons of bits and pieces, and, most important of all, printouts from her cell phone and her computer. Dehan went to get coffee, and I sat at my desk and started sifting through her stuff. It didn't take me long to find Gore's number, Adriel Junker's number, and also Poppy Johnson's. There were lots of others, but these were the only ones she'd called with any kind of regularity or frequency.

The messages from her WhatsApp and her other social media were sobering, and I wondered what Cathy would make of them. Gore had not lied, or even exaggerated, and once again Dehan had nailed it. Clearly she had, as she claimed, a feel for the girl. To say she had been promiscuous was to understate it; though several of the messages made reference to the fact that she expected the guys she had sex with to use a condom, and that she did not inject drugs. But she did have frequent and varied sex, often with people she did not know, and she used drugs, frequently and liberally. She drew the line at injecting, though, as if she felt crossing that border would be a point of no return.

Dehan came back, bearing two large paper cups of coffee, and set them down, one on each of our desks. I tossed her a bunch of printouts I'd already read and telephoned Gore. It rang for fifteen seconds and went to his answering service, so I called Adriel. It rang twice, and a vaguely androgynous voice said, "Who is this?"

"My name is Detective John Stone, of the New York Police Department. Are you Adriel Junker?"

He made a few noises like aborted words and finally said, "Yeah, but like what, why are you calling me?"

I leaned back in my chair and stared at the ceiling for a moment, hoping I might find some patience up there. I didn't.

"I'm calling because we need to talk to you about Sadie Byrne."

More stunted noises followed, and then, "But, like, she's dead."

Dehan winced at what she was reading and looked up at me. I nodded.

"Yeah, Adriel, that's why we need to talk to you."

"Well, I had nothing to do with that."

"But you knew her, didn't you?"

"Yeah, 'course, but . . ."

"So that's why we need to talk to you."

"Yeah but, like, I didn't have anything to do with . . . I mean, you don't think . . ."

"When can you be at the Forty-Third Precinct, Adriel?"

"Uh . . . um . . . uh . . ."

"If it's easier I can send a car for you."

"No! No, like, man, I can come in, uh, in like a while?"

"Make it half an hour."

"Okay, but, like, can I bring a friend?"

I offered Dehan half a smile, but she was engrossed in the printouts and didn't notice.

"Who's your friend?"

"I mean, like, you wouldn't . . ."

"What is your friend's name, Adriel?"

"Poppy? Poppy Johnson?"

"Are you asking me or telling me?"

"No, like, that's her name?"

I rolled my eyes, groaned silently, and shook my head. "Yeah, bring her along too. Half an hour. Don't make me go looking for you."

"No, no, I'll be there, man."

I hung up. Dehan jerked her head at me in a wordless question. I said, "Two for the price of one. Adriel and Poppy, coming together in half an hour. You take Poppy and I'll take Adriel. I fear if you take Adriel you may kill him before the end of the interview."

She leered. "That much fun, huh? I want Adriel! I *want* Adriel!"

"Yeah?" I snorted. "I suggest we swap halfway. We've had Angela and Cathy's perspective on Sadie. These . . ." I pointed at the printouts. ". . . are giving us another view of who Sadie was. What we need from these kids is to know who her closest relationships were and if any of them connected with Chuck . . ."

I was about to correct that, but she cut me short.

"Well, we already know that one of them did. Gore did . . ."

"Exactly."

"So what we want to know is *their* view of what happened that Sunday, and what happened next. Did Gore hold a serious grudge against Chuck? And was there anybody else in their wider group who also connected with Chuck?"

"Correct. Also." I picked up a pencil and wagged it at her. "I am not satisfied with this idea that Chuck was the only man ever in Angela's life."

She blended a smile and a frown on her face and asked me, "Why?"

"Because . . ." I swung my chair back and forth, staring around the large, busy room, wondering why. "Because though she is a little naïve, like her sister, she is not prudish like her sister, and she *is* an attractive woman. I just don't believe that she never had a boyfriend, not a one, until she met Chuck."

She shrugged. "So why would she lie?"

"Exactly. If she'd said to me, 'Oh there was Pete and there was Joe, but I haven't seen them for ten, fifteen, twenty years,' I would not be curious. But she wants us to believe that there was *never* another man in her life, and that makes me wonder why. That means she may be hiding a lover. And *that* would be meaningful."

"Okay, the kids might know something. Unlikely—these kids strike me as the type who are aware only and exclusively of themselves and what's on their damned cell phones. But we can prod them and see if they squeak."

They arrived half an hour later, and I had a sergeant take them up to interview rooms two and three while Dehan and I finished looking through the printouts. Then we went up, and Dehan took Poppy while I went in to talk to Adriel.

When I pushed through the door, he looked up at me. He looked scared. He had scarlet hair cut real short on the right side of his head, but hanging down to his shoulder on the left, with a long, limp fringe that covered his left eye. To say he was skinny would be an understatement. He looked anorexic, and his very pale skin, his baggy blue shirt, skintight jeans, and huge pink boots enhanced that impression and made him look slightly diseased. I offered him a noncommittal smile and sat opposite him at the table.

"Thanks for coming in, Adriel. Did anyone offer you a coffee?"

He ran his fingers through his slick hair and plastered it down on the long side. "I don't drink coffee."

I considered him a moment and decided not to waste my time trying to create rapport.

"You were pretty close with Sadie, right?"

He shrugged. "I guess."

I put both hands palm down on the table and stared at a spot a few inches in front of him.

"You don't know if you were close to her?" I raised my eyes to hold his. "What, you don't remember? You have amnesia? Something happened?"

"No, man . . ."

I gestured at him with my open right hand. "You said you 'guessed' you were close. That means you don't know, you're not sure. If you have to guess it means you don't know. But I *know* that you called each other over a thousand times in the year before she died. That is at least three times a day, every day, for a year. You messaged each other well over three thousand five hundred times, and I happen to know you saw each other pretty much every day. So what is it you are guessing at, Adriel? You don't remember all that?"

His Adam's apple was bouncing up and down like it was trying to escape from his skinny throat. He was giving his head little shakes, repeating, "No, no, man." Finally he got out, "It's like a saying. Yeah, yeah, we were close."

"Saying 'I guess' is the same as saying 'yes'?"

"Yeah, man."

"So what the hell do you say when you want to say, 'I guess'?"

"I dunno, I guess, I guess..."

I closed my eyes and counted to ten. "Let's start again, Adriel, and this time try to say what you mean, and mean what you say. Were you and Sadie close?"

"Yes."

"So how close were you?"

He seemed to shrink. His fingers went through his hair again, and I noticed they were shaking. "I dunno."

"You don't know how close you were? What *do* you know, Adriel?"

"I don't know. I mean, I don't understand your question. I mean, I dunno..."

"Was she your girlfriend? Were you going to get married?" His eyes went wide and his face went crimson. I ignored him and went on. "Did you have sex with each other? Did she have sex with other guys? Did you have sex with other girls? Were you planning to live together...? *How close were you, Adriel?* It is not a difficult question!"

He fumbled. "I... we hung out, you know? Sometimes we made out. We used to have... have..."

"Sex."

"Yeah, like, sex..."

"For God's sake, Adriel! Was it sex or was it like sex?"

"No, yeah, it was . . ."

"Sex!"

"Yeah, sex! We had sex sometimes. But she screwed other guys too, and girls, and I screwed other chicks, it was cool. It's not like before, when . . ."

I nodded and didn't hold back on the irony. "Yeah, I can see we have progressed a long way. So, you were close, you were intimate, you had sex. How about talk?"

The color that had briefly touched his cheeks drained away completely.

"You mean, did we talk . . . ?"

I narrowed my eyes at him. "I am assuming that even you talked, Adriel. What I am asking you is whether you shared a lot of intimate things. Did she talk about her parents, about other friends, the things that upset her, made her happy, her dreams, what she wanted, what she wanted to do, that kind of stuff."

He nodded. "Yeah. She talked a lot about that shit."

"Shit . . ."

"Stuff."

"Okay. We have some important questions coming up, Adriel, so I am going to need you to focus. How did Sadie feel about her parents? How did she feel about her mother and her father?"

"She, like, hated them?" He hesitated, trying to read my face. I made it blank, and he went on. "She . . . like . . . felt . . ." He swallowed. "She said she felt she had no control. That's . . ." He hesitated; he really needed to say "like" again, but he was afraid to. So he swallowed again instead. "The only reason she did drugs, man, was to like feel she was, like, in control."

"She took drugs to feel she was in control."

"Yeah, it was the only way."

I was going to ask him how that worked but decided against it because he might try to explain. Instead I asked, "Is that why she had so many sexual partners? Because that way she felt in control?"

"Yeah. I guess. Me and her. Because our parents never let us do anything, you know?"

"Yeah, let's try and focus on Sadie, shall we?"

"Okay, I'm just, like, saying what it's like for us. So, they were always, like, on top of her? Controlling her? That's what she said."

"What kind of control? Like forcing her to get up in the morning? Go to college, study . . . ?"

"Yeah, exactly, you know: 'You'll never amount to anything.'" He laughed and ran his fingers through his hair again, plastering it down as he did so, and mimicked: "'Look at your dad and everything he has achieved. Don't you wanna be like your dad?'" He laughed again, a nervous, skinny laugh, and his face and neck flushed red. "Uh, nooo?" He shifted his boney ass on the chair. "I mean, right?"

I nodded once. "Yeah, let me see. He is a successful professional, an expert in his field with a good income, who owns his own house and is, actually, largely in control of his life. She was unhappy, probably on her way to being a junkie, frustrated, lost, promiscuous, out of control, had you as her closest friend, and died of AIDS. Yeah, I think I'd rather be like her."

We stared at each other a moment. He did some more nervous swallowing. I said, "What about other people in her life? Like her aunt and uncle, how'd she get on with them?"

His eyes shifted around a bit and he shrugged. "She didn't talk a lot about them."

"Her uncle had a big bust-up with . . ." I looked around the room, sucking on my teeth like I was trying to remember. It took a while, but eventually he said, "Gore."

I snapped my fingers and pointed at him. "Gore! So, who was Gore, and why the big bust-up?"

"Gore was just like one of the guys . . ."

"*Was* he actually one of the guys? Or was he just *like* one of the guys? And, if so, which guy was he like?"

He sighed. "No, man, it's a way of talking. You *know* what I mean."

"No, I don't. Be precise."

"He *was* one of the guys, man. We like . . ." Another sigh. "We hung out together, her, me, Gore, and Poppy."

"So what happened with Gore and Chuck?"

"I don't know." He stroked his hair and hunched one shoulder. "I wasn't there."

"They must have talked about it."

"Yeah . . ." He shrugged one shoulder again. "It was like Chuck went kind of crazy because Sadie came home with Gore, and he started yelling." He went into a kind of listless chant: "'You should have told us you were coming! Now there's not enough food!'" He started giggling. It was a small, silly sound. "And Sadie was like, 'Woah, Chuck, chill, take it easy, we'll dial out for pizza,' but Gore goes, like, kind of crazy? And he starts like swearing? And calling Chuck a motherfucker? Which, you know, to be fair, he should *not* have done. And Gore tells Chuck, 'I can fuck your niece whenever I like,' and Chuck just went crazy and started beating up on him and broke his nose, and his jaw, and like three or four of his ribs."

"So how come Gore didn't report him to the police? He must have gone to the ER, they should have filed a report."

He shrugged. "I dunno, because I wasn't with him? But what he told us was that he just told the doctor he fell down the stairs when he was drunk."

"Why'd he do that?"

"To protect Sadie."

I thought about that for a moment and decided I didn't believe it.

"I need you to think very carefully now, Adriel. Did Gore ever talk about taking revenge? About getting even with Chuck?"

He stared at me for a moment without expression, then nodded and stroked the long side of his hair.

"Yeah, all the time," he said. "He said he wanted to kill him."

SIX

Dehan was looking dubiously into her paper cup. She was leaning by the coffee machine, with her back against the wall, her knee bent, and the sole of her right foot planted against the wall.

"They should call it the black water machine," she said, then looked at me. "You want some hot black water?"

I shook my head. "You make it sound tempting, but no, thanks. Listen, I've been pretty tough on him. He's scared. I don't know if he's just scared because we're cops, or if he has a particular reason to be worried. But I think if you're nice to him he might open up to you."

Her lip curled and her nostrils dilated. "Thanks. Couldn't I have been the bad cop?"

"What about Poppy?"

"She's as thick as two short planks. She doesn't even use words to communicate. Uh? Uh-huh and uh-uh is about the limit. You read about chimps that have a more extensive vocabulary than this kid. What are we doing to our kids, Stone? How are these kids coming out of school, not just unable to read and write, but unable to *think*?"

"I agree, Dehan, but I was actually talking about . . ."

"I know! It just makes me mad, Stone. Schools are supposed to educate, not diseducate!"

"Dehan . . . ?"

She sighed. "I've been tough on her. Just trying to make her *talk*! You know? Like human beings do. I think it had the contrary effect and made her too scared to say anything. However, before you start wagging your finger at me, I got that Sadie had a difficult relationship with her parents, no surprises there, that her parents nagged her a lot to perform better at school, that Chuck was an asshole who was always on at Sadie, telling her to make something of herself, and that at the pre-Christmas lunch he attacked Gore for no reason. Gore is a real sweet guy who wouldn't say 'boo' to a goose. Chuck put him in the hospital and Gore hated him for it."

I nodded. "According to Adriel he said several times he wanted to kill him."

She raised an eyebrow. "Really?"

"Yeah. Okay, you go be sweet and nice to Adriel, see if he'll tell you where Gore is. I'll do the same with Poppy." I hesitated. "These kids seem to need each other for support."

"With legs that skinny, can you be surprised? What's your point?"

"My point, Dehan, is that if Gore did kill Chuck, the chances are these two knew he was going to do it."

She grunted and looked back into the hot black water the machine had given her. "Yeah, I hear you. I'll see what I can get from him."

I left her staring into the cup, pushed open the door, and smiled at the girl sitting at the table. She was scrawny. Her face was pasty. She had very thick, black eyeliner and extremely red lips. I figured she was twenty or twenty-one, but her face was still that of a child. Her mouth was soft and weak, her cheeks very white, and her peroxide hair looked like a wig that had slipped to one side. The black leather jacket and the skinny black pants looked vaguely absurd.

I sat and made an apologetic face.

"I'm sorry to keep you so long. We're nearly done. If we can just clear up a couple of points you can be on your way. Poppy, isn't it?"

"Uh-huh."

I made a mental note not to ask her yes or no questions.

"It must have been very upsetting for you when Sadie died. How long had you known her?"

"Like... since we were kids?"

"A long time."

"Uh-huh."

"And Adriel?"

"Uh?"

"How long have you known Adriel?"

"Ad?"

"Yeah, Ad?"

"Same."

"And Gore, you all knew each other since you were kids?"

She shook her head. "Gore was later. He was like this kinda crazy asshole, always pushing to get in with us, and nobody wanted to know him? But Sadie, like, said he was okay so we, like, said okay too."

She simpered and shrugged, and I laughed like she'd said something funny. Then I made a worried face.

"Chuck was pretty rough on him, huh?"

She made a noise that sounded like "Chah!" which I took to be affirmative.

"How bad was Gore hurt?"

"Uh, like, *pretty* bad? Broke his *jaw*? And his *ribs*?" Her jaw sagged, and she looked at me from under her brows. It was an expression that seemed to suggest I was stupid for asking. I leaned back in my chair, crossed my arms, puffed out my cheeks and blew, and shook my head.

"I mean," I said, like I was not happy at all with the official line, whatever that was. "I can see why Gore was mad at Chuck. Chuck was out of order."

"Way out."

"Way out of order. You can't just attack someone because of something they say."

"Right? There's free speech, right? I mean, Chuck is fucking his wife, and Pat is fucking Sadie's mum, so why shouldn't Sadie and Gore, or me, or Ad . . . ?"

It was more than I had expected, and I was mildly shocked, but I hid it by nodding, shrugging, spreading my hands, and saying, "Right?"

"Right."

"What I don't get, and maybe you can explain this to me, is why Gore didn't go to the cops."

It was the first expression I had seen on her face, and it was one of tolerant amusement. "You don't go to the cops," she said.

"You don't?"

"Uh-uh."

"Not even if somebody breaks your jaw?"

"Uh-uh."

"So what *do* you do?"

"You live with it or you sort it."

"You sort it?"

"Uh-huh."

"What does that mean? How do you sort it?"

"You do what you godda do. You saw what happened to Chuck."

"Did you?"

The question seemed to surprise her. She faltered. "Well, no, but . . ."

I lowered my voice, like I was being conspiratorial and didn't want anybody else to hear. "Are you saying that Gore killed Chuck?"

"He said he was gonna. And Chuck died, didn't he?"

I stared at her a moment, then smiled like I'd seen through her and she was all talk.

"I think Gore was full of bullshit. He has a big mouth, and that was what got him in trouble in the first place."

She was shaking her head. "Uh-uh, uh-uh, he was real mad. It took him a long time to recover from that beating. His ribs would not heal. His jaw just wouldn't get better. He was hobbling around like an old man for months. He couldn't walk right. He was so badly bruised, and his bruises, he showed me, they would not heal. Chuck beat him so bad he nearly killed him. He broke him. Gore really hated him for that. And he told me and Ad, 'First day I can walk straight, I'm gonna go to his house and I am gonna fucking kill that son of a bitch, right in front of his bitchin' wife, so she can watch him die.'"

"He said that?"

"Uh-huh."

"And you believed he was serious?"

"I know he was."

I shrugged and made a face. "Maybe it's true, maybe it's not. Where is he now, Poppy?"

Like my previous question, this one seemed to shock her, as though the cops wanting to find out where a potential killer was was something she had not foreseen. Her mouth went slack and sagged open. She said, "Uh?"

I smiled at her, a smile that was strictly between us.

"Don't worry, you are far too valuable to me. I won't tell him about you. But I need to talk to him, Poppy, for his own sake. It sounds like Gore needs help, real bad."

I saw her hesitate. Her simple mind liked the role I was casting her in, but she wasn't quite there yet. I frowned and cut her short before she could answer. "But one thing, Poppy. You can't tell anyone about this, not even Ad. He looks at Gore and all he sees is a crazy killer. He doesn't see everything that Gore has been through, what drove him to where he is. He doesn't see that he needs help."

She looked like a codfish after a two-hour lesson in Chinese algebra. Her mouth hung slack; her eyes were dull orbs within the black circles of her mascara. I said, "Where is he, Poppy? For his sake as well as yours."

She blinked. "Crotona Avenue and East 178th? He's got a squat there."

"How long has he been there?"

"Like, a year, maybe? Like, just after all the shit happened?"

"How long since you've seen him?"

"Uh, dunno. Few weeks, I guess. Maybe more. Yeah, I think more."

I nodded and smiled at her. "Thanks, Poppy, you've been real helpful. Just hang on here for a bit and I'll go get Ad for you." I shook my head at her. "Don't call Gore, Poppy. That would be obstructing justice in a homicide investigation. You do time for that. We would find out right away, and I would hate for you to get into that kind of trouble after you've been so helpful."

I called a uniform to stay with her and went next door to get Dehan. I knocked and leaned in the door. Adriel was bright pink, furiously smoothing his hair and laughing compulsively. Dehan raised an eyebrow at me and smiled.

"Detective Dehan, can I have a word with you please?"

"I'm kind of busy," she said with severity. "Can it wait?"

Adriel sneered at me. I ignored him and said, "No, it can't. Now, please."

She left him sulking at the table and followed me a few steps down the passage. When we stopped, she said, "He seems pretty sure Gore went after Chuck, but he wasn't with him when he did it. Seems Chuck hurt Gore pretty bad and he took a long time to recover. Drugs will do that to you. Last he knew, he was hanging out at a squat on Crotona and 178th."

"Good, I got exactly the same from Poppy."

"You mean you actually got her to speak? You're one smooth operator, dude."

I smiled. "Hey, either you got it or you don't. I got it, sugar, what can I tell you? Let's go get Gore."

"What about these two?"

"Cut 'em loose. But tell lover boy if he calls Gore and warns him we're looking for him, he'll do time and he'll never see you again."

She snorted. "That'll break his heart."

"Yeah. Tell him to have a meal sometimes too. These kids are walking skeletons. I'll see you downstairs."

Nineteen seventy-five Crotona Avenue was an ugly, white clapboard box on two floors, with a small, littered front yard and an empty lot next door, where there had once been a house that had burned down. There were no drapes on the windows, but on the top floor you could see a faded pink blanket had been nailed up to keep out the light. Dehan pushed open the gate and went to rap on the door while I had a look over the fence round back. There was a backyard, overgrown with weeds. The back door was closed.

When I got back to the front door, Dehan was talking to a red-haired woman in her thirties. She had a stud in her nose, another in her lip, and one that popped up sometimes on her tongue while she spoke. There was a look of defiance in her pale blue eyes.

She was saying, "Why d'you wanna know? You keep harassing us we gonna sue the city."

It was a knee-jerk threat issued without intent. I spoke quietly as I opened the gate and went through, playing a hunch that was growing stronger at every moment.

"We can do this one of two ways, sister. This is a murder investigation. So we could haul you, and anyone else squatting in this house, down to the station and charge you with withholding evidence. Or, we can walk away, apply for a warrant, and leave the man lying behind that curtain upstairs to die. Which will make you responsible for his death."

"What? You can't do that. You're bullshitting me." But she didn't look sure.

"When was the last time you saw him?"

"Uh, I dunno, a week . . ." Her eyes were darting to Dehan and back to me as she thought.

I didn't let her think too much. "How'd he look? Fit, strong, healthy?" Her eyes froze, staring into mine. "Or did he look real sick."

She faltered. I stepped forward and pushed her aside. "Get out of my way, will you?"

I ran up the narrow stairs two at a time. There I found a narrow landing running from front to back. I moved quickly to the door that gave onto the room at the front of the house, where I'd seen the blanket hanging, and hammered on the door. Dehan came up behind me. There was no reply. Behind us a couple of doors opened and wraithlike people peered out, like ghosts peering out of Hades.

I reached down and turned the handle. The door opened. The room was dark. Hazy slashes of light cut the darkness from behind the blanket. For a moment my mind flashed back to Chuck Inglewood's house. A fetid smell of feces, urine, and flatulence made me cover my mouth. I heard Dehan mutter, "Jesus! Again?"

I said, "Call an ambulance," and flipped the switch by the door. A bare bulb came on overhead and cast a limpid glow over the room, barely disturbing the shadows. There was a mattress on the floor against the wall on the right. A figure lay on it, covered with rough blankets, orange and dark gray, the kind of thing you might steal from a homeless shelter. Behind me I could hear Dehan snarling, "Get outta here!" And then, "This is Detective Carmen Dehan, we need an ambulance at Crotona and 178th . . ."

I hunkered down beside the prone form and peeled back the

two blankets. It was a dark-haired man, probably in his early twenties, though you'd be forgiven for believing he was in his seventies. He hadn't shaved for some time and he had a thick stubble covering his face. He had a black sweatshirt on, and the stench coming from under the blankets was overpowering. I moved away, found the john, and vomited.

After a moment I rinsed my mouth and went back. I heaved up the sash window, letting in the light and the air. I covered my mouth with my handkerchief and pulled the blankets off the prone man. He had soiled his pants, and there was urine and feces on the mattress. I took his arm and felt his pulse. It was barely more than a flutter.

Dehan came in. "They want to know what's wrong with him."

I shook my head. "He's unconscious, possibly in a coma. He has a slight pulse and seems to be incontinent. He may have AIDS. Age, early twenties. That's all I got."

She walked out of the room again, barking at whoever was on the other end, and I made an inspection of the room. There wasn't much. A couple of pairs of jeans, some sweatshirts and T-shirts, a leather jacket hanging on the back of the door. In the breast pocket I found a wallet, no ID, no driver's license, no cash, but a cell phone. It was an iPhone 11. I showed it to his face to unlock it and opened his messages. Dehan came back in.

"They're on their way."

I showed her the phone. "It's Gore."

"How did you know this was his room?"

I shrugged. "A hunch. He never really recovered from the beating, did he? He slept with Sadie. I figured maybe his immune system was compromised. Also, they hadn't seen him for a while. He was crazier than the other two, I thought maybe he'd be sicker than them too. And when I saw the blanket over the window, that suggested photosensitivity, his body was packing up . . ." I sighed. "They were all sleeping with each other. If they haven't done it already, those two should get themselves tested."

She jerked her head at Gore's prone form. "You think he'll make it?"

I shook my head. Then I shrugged. "Who knows? But it doesn't seem likely, does it?"

"Not very."

"We're going to be a bit stumped if we can't talk to him."

She nodded, then clamped her lower lip with her teeth and gave her head a small sideways twitch. "You think there's much doubt about what happened?"

"Not really, no . . ."

"But?"

"I still can't *see* it, Dehan. I can see this guy stalking Chuck, I can see him slipping in through the French windows and creeping up the stairs. But I *can't* see Chuck, who had taken this guy to pieces before, just submissively allowing him to stab him in the arms and legs while he tried to phone his wife. Especially as Gore had never really recovered from that first beating. I mean, can you visualize that? I can't."

"No. No, I can't. But there may be factors we're not aware of."

"I guess we'll never know." I sighed.

"What we can be sure of is that we have motive, expressed intention, and opportunity. The only thing we are lacking is the means."

"Yeah, the means. We sure are missing that."

We followed the ambulance to St. Barnabas Hospital. On the way I called Angela Inglewood.

"Yes?"

"Mrs. Inglewood, this is Detective Stone."

"Yes, how can I help you, Detective?"

"We have found Gore." I waited. There was only silence. I went on, "He was living in a squat. When we found him he was very sick, in a coma. We suspect he may have AIDS, and we are looking at the possibility that he was responsible for your husband's murder."

Her voice was barely a whisper. "No . . ."

"What makes you say no, Mrs. Inglewood?"

"Gore? It's just . . ." She paused. "No. I can't believe that he would do that."

"Your husband gave him a very severe beating, from which he never really recovered. I'm going to ask you to give this some thought, Mrs. Inglewood, and if you can think of anything, anything at all that seems relevant, please contact us. Can you do that?"

She was silent again, then asked, "Where is he? What hospital?"

"The St. Barnabas."

"All right. If I think of anything . . . But I think you're making a mistake."

She hung up. At the hospital we asked the doctors to contact us if and when he regained consciousness, and then made our way slowly, silently, and a little despondently back toward the 43rd.

SEVEN

We didn't go to the station house in the end. It was getting late, and I decided to go home instead, via the medical examiner's office at the Jacobi. I'd phoned ahead and told him what I wanted, so he was expecting us when we arrived at the morgue.

"I haven't enough work," was his greeting as we came in. "I need you to make more work for me."

"Hello, Frank."

He glanced at Dehan as he picked up a file from his desk. "Why did you marry him? Isn't he a constant drain on your vitality and morale? I would have advised you not to if you had consulted with me."

"Yeah, you know? He told me he could change."

He sighed and shook his head as he opened the file and leafed through it. "She's beautiful, John, and smart, but she *is* naïve." He winced. "What is it, exactly, you want from me? The cause of death for Chuck Inglewood is not just clear, it is patently obvious. He had two arteries and four major veins cut right through in four places. He was virtually exsanguinated."

Dehan was leaning on the doorjamb. I pulled out the steel tube chair and sat opposite him.

"I know that, Frank, and that is my problem. I can't *see* it."

He stopped leafing and looked at me. "What? You can't see it?" He narrowed his eyes up at Dehan. "Are you not feeding him? Are you depriving him of sex? What's wrong with him?"

"Frank, I'm serious. Chuck Inglewood was a big guy. What . . . ?" I gestured at the file. "Six one? He was tough too. And these places where he was cut, they're awkward to get to. I mean, what kind of a position would you have to be in to get that kind of injury? On the insides of his upper arms, near the armpit, deep cuts, and on the insides of his thighs, even deeper. I can't visualize *how* he got those injuries."

His gaze became abstracted. "Well, I grant you . . ." He studied the pictures in the file for a moment. "What I imagined at the time was that perhaps they were fighting, and as he lifted his arms . . ."

I was shaking my head. "I thought about that too, but, forgive me, Frank, you don't fight much, do you?"

"I'm a doctor, John, a forensic pathologist. What do you think?"

"I know. See, the cuts are all wrong. You don't get cuts like that in a scrap."

"They are very clean, almost surgical. I did note that at the time, in the report."

"If they'd been fighting, moving around, the cuts would have been jagged, uneven. There would have been failed attempts, and, for heaven's sake, *why*? If you're attacking someone, intending to kill them, why cut them there? You have the throat, the neck, the chest, the belly, *the wrists*!"

He shrugged and gave his head lots of little shakes. "That's your department."

"But you *can* tell me what position he would have to be in to have received those cuts."

He read over a couple of pages, stuck out his chin a couple of times, and said, "Well, yes." He looked up at me. "I suppose, now that you say it, he would have to have been lying down."

Dehan screwed up her face and said, "*Lying down?*"

And I flopped back in my chair and said, "I knew it."

Dehan stared at me. "What do you mean, you knew it?"

"That's why I couldn't see it. He was lying down."

"So . . ." She wandered out to the autopsy room and stared down at one of the tables. "He's lying down, taking a nap after lunch. That makes sense."

I got up and followed her out. Frank came after us. She turned and grabbed him by the collar of his white coat. "Frank, get on the table, lie down."

His eyes said he was alarmed. "Why me? Why not him?"

"He's too big. Quit griping and lie down." He clambered on the table and lay flat. Dehan shook her head. "No, uh-uh, people don't lie like that unless they're dead, Frank. Fetal position, spooning with your imaginary wife, only relaxed, right?"

He maneuvered himself on his side, with his right hand under his cheek, his lower leg bent, and the top one slightly straighter. She nodded. "Yeah, see?" She turned to me. "He's lying like that, facing the window, away from the door, having a nap after lunch. He's got what the Italians call *abbiocco*. The sleepiness you get after lunch."

"Thanks, I know what *abbiocco* is."

"Gore slips in through the open French windows, just like we said, but he does not encounter Chuck. He encounters nobody, so he creeps up the stairs, slips into the bedroom, and sees Chuck lying just like that. Now!"

She grabbed a saw from the instruments table. Frank stared at her in alarm.

"Be careful with those things, they are extremely sharp!"

She ignored him. "Think about it! In that position, all those places you mentioned—neck, chest, wrists—all awkward to get to. But his inner thigh is exposed. Now, remember, he wants to punish this guy, because he has never recovered from the beating he gave him. So he plunges the knife deep into his inner thigh, a single, clean wound that cuts right into his artery and his vein. Then he pulls out the knife and Chuck starts to bleed out.

"So what does Chuck do? First he grips at the wound to try and stop the bleeding, but he is losing blood fast, and Gore pushes him back and stabs him in the other thigh. By now Chuck is too weak to fight back. His heart is pounding hard in panic and the blood is rushing out of his wounds. Gore, the sick son of a bitch, gives him his phone. 'Call your wife,' and while Chuck is speed-dialing her, he makes the cuts on his arms. Then he leaves."

Frank looked sidelong at her. "It's a viable theory. Are we done here?" He slid off the table and straightened his coat. "It is a viable theory, and certainly the wounds could be consistent with that. And to be perfectly honest"—he looked at me and shrugged—"I can't think of another explanation. You're quite right, the wounds are bizarre, and if I'm not mistaken, that was half the reason Reynolds gave up on the case."

I grunted. Dehan scrutinized my face. "What?"

I ran it through in my head, the way she'd described it. In a case that was crazier than most, it made some kind of crazy sense. Anyone else would have jumped him and stabbed him in the heart, but these freaky, skinny kids with their weird way of doing things might just do it like that. Even so, there were things she hadn't explained.

"Nothing," I said. "Weird case. I guess we'll never really know for sure, but that does seem the most likely explanation. So far."

Frank nodded, then shrugged. "Most likely and perhaps only, Stone. Mind if I get on with my job now?" He went back toward his office and stopped just as he was going through the door. "Oh, I told Joe you were coming over and he said he had found blood in the bathroom. Tiny residues. He said to call him."

I called him as we came out into the parking lot and headed for the car. I put it on speaker, and Dehan fell into step beside me. It rang twice, and he answered.

"Stone, my man! I haven't had a chance to do anything with it yet. I just thought you'd like to know."

"Only in the bathroom?"

"Yeah, nothing in the bedroom. The bathroom floor and the exposed part of the bedroom floor were very clean compared to the rest of the bedroom, the hall, et cetera. The traces we found, and there were quite a few of them, were around the rim of the tap, where it connects with the bathtub, and in the grout between the tiles above the bath. There is no way of testing that blood, John. It may well be unrelated. Mrs. Inglewood might have cut herself shaving her legs, one of them might have slipped and fallen . . ."

"But she'd have to cut herself pretty badly, right?"

"Yes, this is the remains of blood that has been cleaned up, and by its distribution there was a fair bit of it. However, what I am trying to say is that there is no way of showing that this blood was from Mr. Inglewood, that it is the same blood that is on the bed. We can't establish that. The specks are minute and mixed with grout."

"What about the sheets and the duvet, and the stuff in the washing machine?"

"Haven't got to them yet, but I'll let you know as soon as I do. Weird case, huh?"

"A bit weird, yeah."

I hung up. We'd come to where the Jag was parked under the plane trees, and I threw Dehan the keys. She caught them left-handed and leaned on the roof of the car. The sun was slipping toward evening and a dappled, golden light lay across her face.

"You'd better tell me or you're going to be a pain in the ass all evening, and I'd like to enjoy my dinner."

"He didn't do it."

She smiled. It was not a happy smile. It was the kind of smile that says, "I'd like to knock your head off right now." She looked down at the roof of the car and drummed on it with her fingers. She spoke without looking up.

"How do you know he didn't? I mean, I can understand you saying, 'I don't believe he did it,' or, 'I don't think he did it,' or even, 'I'm not convinced he did it.' But not good old John Stone, no. Sensei John Stone says, 'He didn't do it.'"

I leaned opposite her and looked up at yellowing leaves. Then I shook my head and shrugged my shoulders at her. "He didn't do it, Dehan. It's not about my ego. It's a simple fact. Think about it. He never recovered from the beating Chuck gave him because he was HIV positive. His health has been declining ever since, for the last eighteen months or two years. There is no way that guy, in his declining condition, stalked Chuck. And there is absolutely no way he would have put himself at risk of another beating by going into Chuck's house alone to confront him. He talked about killing him, sure, but that was all hot air, bluster, bravado . . . fantasy. He knew he was dying, and he knew it was Chuck who had killed him, just as much as the HIV. But there is no way, realistically, *no way* that he could ever have confronted Chuck and killed him."

She looked away and did a lot of slow nodding. In the end she sighed and shrugged and said, "Yeah, I agree, it is hard to believe. But we both speculated that he might have been going through a psychotic episode. God knows he sounds crazy enough. A lethal combination of hatred, drugs, and despair." She gave a small laugh. "Let's face it, Stone, there isn't another explanation. You said from the start that those wounds were inflicted by somebody who wanted to punish him, somebody who was crazy. You were right. And Gore ticks both boxes and fits the bill."

I gave my head a couple of small shakes. "No, there's more."

There was an edge of despair to her voice when she asked, "More? What, Stone?"

I drummed on the roof of the car with my hands and opened the door. "The blood," I said. "The blood."

She slid behind the wheel, slammed the door, and fit the key in the ignition. "What about the blood?"

"We'll have to wait and see."

"Oh, that's your answer? We'll have to wait and see? That's your explanation, for 'the blood'?"

I closed my eyes and rested my head on the back of the seat. We drove in silence the short distance to Haight Avenue, parked, climbed out of the Jag, and walked into the house without speaking. Dehan made spaghetti Bolognese and opened a bottle of wine, and I made a fire, even though we didn't need one, and two martinis, extra dry. Eventually, after dinner, we fell asleep on the sofa, watching *The Maltese Falcon*.

Dehan was up at six. She showered and, while I followed suit, she dressed and made bacon and eggs and rye toast, and a pot of strong, black coffee. The smells drew me down the stairs while I was still pulling on my clothes, and as I was kissing her good morning, my cell rang. It was an undisclosed number.

"Yeah, Detective Stone."

I could hear breathing, not heavy, rather shallow and rapid, as though in fear. I said, "Who is this? If you're in trouble say something, or call 911."

That made Dehan look up and watch. There was a small intake of breath, then the line went dead. I called the station.

"Yeah, this is Stone, I need a call traced."

I gave them the details and hung up. Dehan was dishing up the food. I collected the plates and took them to the table. My mind was beginning to race. She said, "You going to tell me?"

I sat. "Nobody spoke. I'm pretty sure it was a woman. The breathing was light and shallow. She gave a little gasp and hung up." I looked at my watch. "It's six fifty. Pretty early to be up calling people."

She filled my cup. "You think you know who it is. I can tell."

I held her eye a moment. "I think it was Cathy Byrne."

Her eyebrows said she was surprised. The rest of her face said she was eating breakfast. We did that in silence for a while before she leaned back in her chair, sipping her coffee.

"You know what, Stone? I get the feeling that in that family they're all a bit neurotic. She was probably just calling to beg you not to be too tough on Gore. Like she did when we saw her."

I didn't answer, and by the time we were clearing the table my cell rang again. It was the station.

"Good morning, Detective. The call you received came from a landline registered at nineteen eighty-four Powell Avenue, the Bronx, to a Mr. Patrick Byrne."

I thanked him and hung up. Dehan jerked her chin at me in a mute question.

"The call came from the Byrnes house. From the landline."

She picked up a tea towel and started drying her hands. "So either the caller has no idea of modern technology, or she wanted you to know where the call came from."

"What would make her do that at six fifty a.m.?"

She didn't answer right away but grabbed her jacket and slipped it on. "Ask her."

"I plan to."

I called from the car at just before seven thirty a.m. The voice that answered was not Cathy's. It was a man's, but oddly neutral, almost androgynous.

"Yes, who is this?"

"This is Detective John Stone, of the New York Police Department. I received a call from your landline at six fifty this morning. Nobody spoke, and the number was undisclosed. I'd like an explanation."

He was quiet so long I began to think he wasn't going to answer me, but finally he said, "Detective John Stone. You were here yesterday. You are investigating Sadie's rape."

"Who am I speaking to?"

"This is Dr. Patrick Byrne, Detective. This is my house, and you spoke to my wife."

"Was it she who called me this morning?"

"I really don't know, but it is entirely likely. We were discussing your visit, last night, and . . ." He sighed, like he found his own voice boring. "She told me about your line of questioning. So I pointed out certain facts that she had omitted to mention to you."

"What facts, Dr. Byrne?"

"Look, I have a meeting at the university and I cannot be late. I have to be in Queens at eight thirty. But I suggest you speak to Cathy this morning, and I will try to get back here by ten, in case I can add anything to the dialogue. I am aware that she is not always very"—he paused and sighed, then said with emphasis—"*coherent*."

"Dr. Byrne, why did this information, whatever it is, not come out in the original investigation?"

"I can't really answer that, Detective. I wasn't aware of it back then. I can only imagine it did not seem relevant at the time—I'm not sure it is now—and the detectives who had charge of the case did not pursue that line of inquiry. Look, I really have to go. I'll try to be back by ten if you are still here."

He hung up without waiting for a reply.

Dehan raised an eyebrow at the phone, then used it to look at me.

"What the hell's that about?"

"Certain *facts* that she had omitted to mention . . ."

"Related to our line of questioning."

"Our line of questioning was, had Angela had any other men in her life, and could Cathy think of anyone who might want to hurt Chuck Inglewood."

She nodded then kind of shrugged. "Which led us to Gore."

We were on White Plains, headed for the 43rd, but when we got to the expressway overpass I took a left onto McGraw Avenue and then right onto the Hugh J. Grant Circle via Metropolitan Avenue. Dehan glanced at me.

"You going straight there?"

"Why not? Let's not give her time to think it over too much. She didn't tell us yesterday, and she didn't speak this morning; that tells me she's not crazy keen to tell us about whatever it is Patrick reminded her about. Let's strike while the iron is hot."

I took the expressway as far as Pugsley and turned south, then negotiated the one-way system and entered Powell from the west.

I parked in the shade of the big green maple and climbed out of the Jag, feeling inexplicably mad. Dehan came round and joined me, and as I made for the steps she put a hand on my arm.

"Stone?"

"Yeah?"

"You okay?"

I frowned. "Sure. Why?"

"I don't know. This case, it seems to have got under your skin."

I shook my head. "No." I tried out a smile which I didn't feel. "Shall we go in?"

I climbed the steps and rang the bell. It opened after a short while, and Cathy Byrne gave a small gasp when she saw us.

"Oh!" she said. "I, um . . ."

"You called."

I said it with absolutely no expression. She went to answer, but my expressionless face told her there was no point. The three of us stood staring at each other for a few seconds, till I said, "Can we come in?"

"Yes, yes, I suppose you'd better." She followed us into the living room. We sat without being asked, and she dithered in the middle of the floor. "I was just making some coffee. Shall I . . . ? Will you . . . ?"

Dehan smiled. "Thank you."

She joined us after a couple of minutes, with a tray loaded with cups, saucers, milk and sugar, and a pot of coffee that smelt strong. As she started to pour, I said, "It was pretty early, six fifty. Why didn't you speak?"

She handed Dehan a cup, screwed up her eyes, and then gave a nervous laugh.

"Well, that was it, really. I realized what time it was and hung up immediately. I don't know what I was thinking!"

She appealed with a laugh to Dehan, who smiled and sipped. I watched her and waited without expression until she'd stopped laughing. Then I said, without any particular emphasis, "Stop lying, Cathy."

"Oh, no, I wasn't . . ."

"What did you want to tell me this morning?"

"No, it was, I was just wondering about Gore, whether you had . . ."

"Stop lying."

I saw tears in her eyes. Dehan flicked me a frown and said, "Cathy, we spoke to your husband this morning. He told us about your conversation last night. You have to level with us. If there is evidence you have not shared, innocent people could get into trouble, not least you."

She had been staring at the palm of her left hand. Now she looked up, wide-eyed. "Me?"

There was something surprisingly tender in Dehan's face when she sat forward with her elbows on her knees.

"Cathy, withholding evidence in a murder inquiry is a very serious matter. Quite aside from the fact that it could lead us to arrest an innocent person, or allow a killer to walk free, you could wind up in prison."

She shook her head, appealing to us each in turn with a face on the verge of tears. "But it's really nothing."

"If that's so," I said, "then there is no reason for you not to tell us, and in any case, Cathy, you have to let us decide whether it is something or nothing. That's our job, not yours, and it is what we are trained to do."

She flopped back in her seat and laid her hands on her lap.

"Well, I suppose I have to tell you now anyway, don't I?"

"What was it your husband pointed out to you last night?"

She sat forward again, poured me a cup of coffee, and handed it over.

"I told you yesterday that Angela had never had an affair, and that Chuck was the only man she had ever been with. Well, that wasn't strictly true."

EIGHT

I ARCHED MY EYEBROWS IN AN "I TOLD YOU SO" SORT OF way and showed them to Dehan, who grunted softly and sat back in her chair, looking into her coffee. Cathy made a crying face and tilted her head to one side, gazing at the coffeepot like it was being unkind to her.

"But, it was over *twenty years* ago! And we all agreed never to discuss it again. It can't possibly have anything to do with Sadie's . . ." Her lips worked but nothing came out till she said, ". . . unfortunate business."

An unreasonable irritation made me say, "You mean her rape?"

"Well, yes. Or Chuck's murder."

"Why don't you tell us what happened, Cathy, and we'll see."

She took a deep breath and slumped her shoulders.

"It was at least twenty years ago. I wasn't even pregnant yet, though Pat and I were married. Angela was with Chuck, they were married too, and they'd been trying for a baby, but the Lord hadn't blessed them in that way. Then, it was awful really, very embarrassing all round. They'd both been having tests, and suddenly, out of the blue, the doctors told Angela she was pregnant. Well, we were all celebrating and rejoicing that the Lord had blessed them with a child, when Chuck got the results from the clinic he'd been to, and they said that he was impotent. That he could not have babies. Well, you can imagine that he was furious. And it turned out that Angela had been having an affair with a man at work."

My mind leapt ahead, trying to see all the implications. I asked her, "How did Chuck react?"

"He was devastated. And raging."

"Obviously. But what did he do? How did he *react*?"

"At first he was furious. They had a huge row. It was so bad that Angela came and stayed with us. At first she wouldn't tell us what it was about. And it was years before we told Pat all the details. He doesn't like to get involved anyway. But eventually, you know, sisters, she told me. She said she was going to have an abortion, but I told her she couldn't do that. She was out of her mind with worry, thinking she was going to lose Chuck, crying her eyes out every night . . ."

Dehan asked, "How long was she here?"

"A week."

"And Patrick didn't want to know what was going on?"

"No, not really. He has always been far more interested in his work than anything else." She simpered. "As long as we didn't bother him, he didn't bother with us."

I said, "So what happened?"

She closed her eyes again and took a deep breath.

"We decided that the only thing she could do was to go away, have the baby, and leave it at an orphanage, give it up for adoption."

Dehan frowned, hard. "What about the father?"

Her eyebrows shot up, and a wave of indignant red washed her cheeks.

"Oh! *She* wanted to go and tell him! As if the problem were not complicated enough! She wanted to go and tell the man, not only that she was pregnant with his baby, but that she was going to give it up for adoption!"

I saw Dehan draw breath and gave her a warning look. I asked, "And did she?"

"No! Thank heavens I managed to persuade her not to. Can you *imagine* the chaos that would have ensued? It doesn't bear thinking about. No." She shook her head. "Thankfully, after a few days, on the fifth day, I think, Chuck called on the telephone and then came around. They talked, and Angela was suitably, and sincerely—I think—remorseful and begged him for forgiveness. He was big enough to say that he would bring up the child as though it were his own. But she insisted—and I think he was relieved—that she would go away to have it and give it up to be adopted."

The room went silent. Cathy looked like she'd got a heavy load off her shoulders and sagged back slightly in her chair. Dehan was looking up at the ceiling, like she had her thoughts displayed up there and she was organizing them. I said:

"So who was this guy?" Cathy drew breath, and I knew she was going to lie, so I cut her short. "Don't tell me you don't know, Cathy. I've been around long enough to know that sisters tell each other everything in these situations, and you and Angela are no exception. Who is he?"

"He was her boss." She looked at me and shook her head. There was a hint of despair about the gesture. "It was over *twenty* years ago." I didn't respond, so she went on. "She had a secretarial job at a graphic design company, Copes and Sanders, on Walton Avenue, just by the court. She was secretary to one of the partners. It was a nice job, and they treated her really well, raised her salary a couple of times in the first few months, gave her bonuses when they got new clients, took her out to lunch . . ."

She had begun to smile, but the smile faded. "Of course, at first we thought it was just that they appreciated her as a good worker. Then we realized. She had been getting close with Sebastian."

Dehan said, "Sebastian?"

"Her boss, Sebastian Copes. She and Chuck had been having

a difficult time. It was very stressful for them. Angela desperately wanted a child, and he was working so hard setting up his business. They were under a lot of stress, and I guess Sebastian made her feel good. He flattered her, told her she was a wonderful worker, took her out for lunch . . . Well, pretty soon one thing led to another."

Dehan grunted. "It always does. That's why you have to stay away from the one thing, to avoid the other."

I glanced a smile at her and turned back to Cathy. "So what happened?"

She took a deep breath. "I told her she should send in a letter of resignation, apologize, say she was very sorry, but some personal issues had come up and she could no longer go into work. But she insisted she could not do that. She had to go personally and tell Sebastian that it was all over between them. I made her swear she would not mention the baby, and she agreed that that would be a stupid thing to do. Then we spoke to a few clinics around the country and found one in Portland . . ."

Dehan arched her brows high. "Oregon? You went all the way to Oregon?"

Cathy smiled and tilted her head gently to one side. "No, Maine. The one in Oregon is named after ours. We are originally from New England, the Ryans. It's very nice up there. Our Portland is named for Portland Isle, in Dorset, England. Nice people, in Portland." She blinked a few times after her display of erudition, then said, "The Westbrook Private Maternity Clinic. They were very sweet and arranged everything."

"They arranged the orphanage?"

"Yes. Well, we had an old friend working at the orphanage, Mary Finch, so that kind of influenced Angela's decision too. We made an excuse that she was going to visit family in New England, and she went just before the bump started to show. Chuck used to go visit most weekends, and then in late November, twenty-sixth of November, 1997 . . ." She giggled at Dehan, who reciprocated. "My God! Last century! Seems like yesterday, baby was born. She never got to hold him, or touch him. They mustn't bond, you see. He was taken away, and she came home, and that was the end of it."

Dehan made a lopsided face that wasn't quite a smile and looked at me like she was returning my earlier "told you so." I ignored her and asked Cathy, "So did Angela ever have any more contact with Sebastian Copes?"

She shook her head. "No. What she wanted above all else was to heal her relationship with Chuck. I mean, he was a good man, and she really did love him. He had a bit of a temper, but most of the time he controlled it, and he *never* directed it at family. He was a real family man; it was a tragedy they never had kids. And I think she felt very, very guilty about what she'd done. He didn't deserve that." She shook her head. "While he was out breaking his back working to make a future for them, she was sleeping with another man. That is not right."

I sighed and ran my fingers through my hair. "Cathy, you realize we will have to discuss this with Angela."

She looked queasy. "Do you have to? She will never forgive me. I gave her my word I would never tell a soul. Will you give me a day or two to try and persuade her to tell you herself?"

I glanced at Dehan. She gave a tiny shrug. I nodded. "Not a day or two, Cathy. This is a murder investigation. You have till this afternoon."

Dehan added, "You did the right thing, Cathy. You may well be right and there is no connection at all. But it's always best to play it safe."

We thanked her for the coffee, and she saw us to the door. Out in the bright morning sunshine, when we'd heard the door close behind us, Dehan pulled the passenger door open and looked at me across the roof of the car.

"You satisfied?"

I smiled and climbed in. She got in beside me, we slammed the doors, and I turned the key in the ignition. The big old engine growled.

"Satisfied? What with?"

"Stone, this is a wild goose chase."

"What is?"

"Sebastian Copes is. Why would he, after twenty years, suddenly decide he has a grudge against Chuck?"

"I don't know." I rolled to the end of Powell and turned left onto Pugsley.

"You turned left."

"Yes."

"Stone, this is us chasing a wild goose who is chasing a red herring."

"How do you know?"

"Because there is no motive!"

I wound my way to Virginia Avenue and returned to the Hugh J. Grant Circle, then came off for the Cross Bronx Service Road. Once we had settled into the flow, I glanced at her again and said, "How do you know?" She spread her hands in a kind of mock desperation at my blindness to what was self-evident. I said, "I'm not saying you're wrong, Dehan. I just wonder how you know."

She turned away and looked out the window. I gave her a moment, and when I saw she wasn't going to answer, I went on. "It's obvious? It's self-evident? How many cases went cold under those labels? Yes, Gore had a powerful motive to want Chuck dead. But he was also probably physically incapable of committing the murder, and we have no witnesses and no physical or forensic evidence tying him to the Inglewoods' house that day. What we *do* have is a very incongruent set of circumstances that are as yet unexplained, concerning the blood. I don't know what's wrong, Dehan, but something is. Very. So I want to keep digging."

She sat in silence, with her thumb pressed against her lower lip. After a bit she turned to face me.

"Okay, I agree. There are things we can't explain, and in this particular case, given that Gore may not emerge from his coma, maybe we will never be able to explain them. But, just as an example of how it might have gone down, let's say Gore slips into the house. Remember, this is almost two years ago, so his AIDS has not progressed so much. He is angry, perhaps in a rage. This guy is given to extreme behavior. So he goes in, sprints up the stairs, bursts in the room, and performs his attack in seconds. And while Chuck is bleeding out on the bed, Gore goes into the bathroom and showers off the blood. It need only take a minute. Then, with a wet towel he wipes the blood off the floor and leaves. He has no idea that Chuck has been calling his wife, and the cops. Over and done in less than five minutes. Stop smiling like that!"

"Okay, yes, it's possible—just! And maybe we'll have to settle for that. But, Dehan, we'd be settling, because you know as well as I do that that is *not* a satisfactory explanation."

"Why?" She raised her hand. "No, sorry, open question. What is it that makes it unsatisfactory?"

"Remind me," I told her. "What is Gore's motive?"

She looked away. "Revenge."

"Revenge for precisely what?"

"For the beating,"

"The beating which left him for months in extreme pain, with unhealed injuries that he knew would never truly heal. He *hates* Chuck. And he has satisfied this powerful need for revenge in a matter of seconds. He doesn't linger and enjoy it, or vent his passion. Why? Because, in this fevered state of mind, he is more interested in taking a shower than in making Chuck suffer. And let me highlight something else, while we're at it. When he dashes in and sprints up the stairs, yes, his AIDS is not as advanced as when we found him, but he *is* crippled with fractured ribs that will not heal, and a fractured jaw which was also unhealed and must have been constant agony. Not a satisfactory explanation."

I glanced at her. Her gaze was lost out the window. I said:

"I haven't got an explanation, Dehan. Neither have you. That's why we're looking for one."

She sighed and nodded but didn't say anything.

We came off onto East 163rd Street and followed it onto 161st at Elton Avenue. After the Supreme Criminal Court and the county clerk's office we finally turned left onto Walton Avenue. I glanced at my watch. It was just before nine. I pulled into an empty space outside the county clerk's and got out. Opposite was the Court Deli restaurant, a short terrace of shops, all called Court-something, and then 853, a big 1930s six-story yellow-brick, with a fire escape zigzagging down the front. There was a brass plaque beneath the number, and as I drew closer I saw it read, "Copes & Sanders, Graphic Design."

There was an arched doorway framed in dark wood, and plate glass doors with brass handles. Beside the door was an intercom system with twelve bells. Number ten, on the fifth floor, was Copes and Sanders. I pressed it. It made an ugly electronic noise, and a voice you could describe as debonair spoke from behind me.

"There won't be anybody there." I turned. He was tall, six-three or -four, and lanky in expensive designer jeans, a two-hundred-dollar shirt with pink stripes, and an Armani linen jacket. His floppy blond hair had cost two hundred dollars to cut and had then had the gray dyed out of it. He pulled off his Versace sunglasses and smiled at me the way benign superior men smile at amusing inferior men.

"Nobody arrives before nine thirty," he went on. "Except me. Can I help you?"

I didn't return the smile because I had decided I didn't like him.

"Maybe you can." I showed him my badge. "I'm Detective John Stone." I pointed across the road where Dehan was crossing toward us. "That's my partner, Detective Carmen Dehan. I'm looking for Sebastian Copes."

He was watching Dehan the way a hungry spaniel watches a scoop full of food. He wrenched his eyes away from her and smiled at me again. "Yes, I am Sebastian Copes. How can I help you?"

NINE

Dehan joined us, holding up her badge, and I spoke while he inspected her body.

"We'd like to talk to you about Angela Inglewood."

He blinked a few times and smiled as he withdrew his gaze from Dehan's legs.

"I'm sorry, did you just say . . . ? May I see your badge again?"

He took it in his hands and made an elaborate show of inspecting it in detail, squinting at it up close, like it must be a joke that we were cops. Dehan sighed noisily.

"Are we done with the theatrics, Mr. Copes?"

He glanced at her without humor and handed me back my badge. "You're for real. Good God! What has that bitch done now?"

I said, "Is there somewhere we can talk? We need to ask you some questions."

He gave his head a lot of short, jerky shakes. "No!" There was an almost hysterical edge to his voice. "No, there isn't somewhere we can talk because you need to ask me some questions! *You . . .*" He leaned forward and pointed at my chest with a long finger. "*You* and *you . . .*" He turned and did the same to Dehan. "*You . . .*" He pointed at us both in turn. ". . . *need* to ask me questions. I do not *need* you to ask me any questions. I, frankly, could not give a *damn* about that gold-digging *bitch* and her lies. Whatever it is" —he waved both hands elaborately in the air—"*I-just-don't-care!* Is that . . . Now I am just going to ask in case I have been vague or misleading, *the way she fucking was*! Is that *clear* enough for you?"

He stepped toward the door pulling a set of keys from his jacket pocket. Dehan's eyes had narrowed, and a darkness seemed to have settled on her brow. I smiled.

"Misleading?" He stopped and stared at me over his shoulder. I shook my head. "That wasn't what I had heard."

He laughed. "Oh, no! Oh no you don't! I am not falling for that one. You may have heard whatever you may have heard. I *know* what happened. See, I was *there*."

"Yeah, I bet you were. You lured a vulnerable, young married woman into an extramarital affair, and then you dumped her when things got complicated."

Dehan's eyes were like dinner plates, and she was staring at me with all of both of them.

Copes had frozen while he listened to me. Now he turned, the keys still in his right hand, both hands held wide, his mouth trying and failing to produce *W* words as he shook his head in disbelief.

"I did *what now*? What has she *told* you? *Vulnerable?* That whore? *Married? Dumped her?* Let me tell you something, Mr. Detective. That *bitch* maneuvered herself into my office as my secretary, she told me her husband had abandoned her for some Colombian floozy he'd met in a bar and called him *papito*. She said he had left her broke and unable to meet her mortgage payments. I, like the great *schmuck* that I am, raised her salary *twice*! To try and help her out." He jabbed his finger savagely and repeatedly at the sunny morning beyond his building. "*She!*" He elongated the *ee* sound. "*Sheeee* seduced *meee*! Not the other way around. And then one fine day she comes into the office on Monday morning, after taking a week off sick, and . . ."

He stopped dead, scowling down at me. I said, "And what?"

"... And announces that she is leaving, that our relationship is over, that she is going to try and make it work with her husband."

"Is that all she told you?"

"Yes, what else? It was over. And she had the *gall*—the sheer *gall*—to tell me she had come in person to tell me, as though I should be grateful for that. She cried. The bitch actually *cried* in my office, as though *I* should be comforting *her*, then she got up and left."

Dehan was frowning hard now. She said, "Are you telling us, Mr. Copes, that you were actually serious about Angela?"

"Serious? *Serious?* Are you kidding me? I was *insane* about her! I wanted to marry her. I told her, '*Get a fucking divorce!* I'm a fucking *millionaire!* An apartment in town and a house in the country! You'll live in *luxury!*' But no, she played me, had her fun, and went back with her fucking plumber!"

She nodded. "That's got to hurt. It was twenty years ago, but you're still pretty mad."

The only way to describe his expression was a sneer. He sneered down at Dehan and said, "No, little lady, I am not mad. I happen to be a man who expresses his feelings without restraint. That makes me an exceptionally good lover. A fact you are welcome to confirm for yourself anytime you want."

I snarled, "Watch your mouth, Copes!"

But he ignored me. "I got over Angela a long time ago. Does you two turning up and reminding me all about her make me mad? Yes, it does. And I will never forgive that bitch for her callous, coldhearted betrayal. But am I over her? Yes. One hundred fucking percent. Now, kindly leave me alone, and if you want my testimony for anything, get a fucking court order, or a subpoena or whatever you fucking need! Because I don't *give* a damn about Angela, and I have nothing more to say to you!"

He turned, and with a little too much fumbling to preserve his dignity, he unlocked the door and strode in, headed for the elevators. The door closed behind him, and he vanished from view.

Dehan was staring at me with narrowed eyes and a hint of a smile playing on her lips. "He arrived in an Aston Martin," she said.

"I can't fault his taste in cars, or women for that matter, though he seems to have gone a little overboard with Angela."

She stepped away onto the sidewalk, and I followed her. She shrugged, her hands in her jeans pockets, her hair tied in a long, loose ponytail, and her shades perched on the top of her head. I was possessed suddenly of an almost uncontrollable desire to take hold of her and kiss her. But fortunately she glanced over her shoulder and smiled.

"You don't know what she looked like twenty years ago. She would have been in her early twenties, maybe rebelling."

I made no comment and followed her to the car, where she placed her backside on the hood with her hands between her knees and considered me. I said:

"Well, one thing we have learned is that Angela Inglewood, née Ryan, was certainly not the saintly person she and her sister like to portray. Things were rough with her and Chuck, and she was not above a little gold-digging and fib-telling."

She nodded, then gave her head a sideways twitch. "Perhaps more to the point, Stone, your alternative suspect, Sebastian Copes, A, seems to have been taken totally by surprise by our visit, and B, held a much bigger grudge against Angela than he did against Chuck. I am sorry, but I just do not see this guy sneaking up the stairs and stabbing Chuck in the thigh. It's just . . . no."

"I agree."

"You agree?"

"Yeah, but the fact that Copes didn't do it doesn't mean that Gore did. Likewise, the fact that Gore didn't do it doesn't mean that Copes did. There are many more ways to skin this cat. Just off the top of my head, Copes can afford to pay for somebody to do the dirty work for him. I'm not saying he did, I'm just saying it is one of many possible permutations. What is undeniable is that Copes was badly hurt and has a problem with self-control."

"Sure, but where does that take us?"

I grinned at her. "That's the best question you've asked all morning, Little Grasshopper. Where does it take us?" I stepped over and sat next to her with my arms crossed over my chest. "Was there anything, Dehan, anything at all that struck you as odd in the way he spoke, or the things he said?"

She looked up at me and smiled, and leaned gently against my arm. "You mean apart from everything, Sensei?"

"Yes, I mean apart from everything. Think, was there one particular thing that caught your attention?"

"Okay, big guy, hit me, what was I supposed to notice?"

I thought for a moment. "The fact that she turned up in person to tell him their relationship was over, that she was going to try to make it work with her husband, and that she had the *gall* . . ." I smiled at her. "The *gall* to expect him to be grateful."

She shook her head. "Why is that unusual? It's exactly what Cathy told us she'd done."

"Yup, pretty much."

"So? You're being cryptic, Stone. You know it drives me crazy when you do this."

"It just struck me as odd. Look, you asked me what next. Well, here is what I think we do next. We go and we talk to Angela . . ."

"You told Cathy you'd give her till this afternoon."

"Yeah . . ." I stared at her face for a long moment. It was a nice face to stare at. "I am not sure that's such a good idea. I think we need to go talk to her right away. Chances are, Dehan, Cathy has already spoken to her sister by now. Either way, we can call her and see."

"Stone." She put a hand on my shoulder. "I gotta tell you, I don't really know what you hope to get from Angela except corroboration of what Cathy already told us."

I nodded, ignoring what she was saying. "We also need to

confront Copes with the fact that Angela was pregnant with his son."

"What *for*, Stone?"

I took a big breath and sighed. "Because, because, because, because . . . I need to make a phone call."

I pulled my cell from my jacket and called the inspector.

"John, good of you to call. How are you? Working hard?"

"Yes, sir, listen, I need something done fast, and I wonder if you have any connections . . ."

"Well, John, as long as we are not circumventing the law." There was a smile in his voice, and also a caution.

"No, sir, nothing like that." I stood and took a couple of steps away, then turned to look at Dehan as I spoke. "We're looking at the Chuck Inglewood case."

"Doesn't ring any immediate bells."

"Well, it has emerged that the victim's wife became pregnant and gave the child up for adoption, and it may be that the adoption itself, whoever adopted him, may have some bearing on the victim's murder . . ."

"Oh, yes, I see that could be the case . . ."

"Trouble is, the kid was put up for adoption in Maine, and I need that orphanage to talk to me . . ."

"And you want me to pull strings with the Maine Police Department, the orphanage, and if necessary the judiciary."

"Without circumventing due process, sir, yes. But I have a feeling this might be quite an urgent matter."

He made a noise that said he was dubious. "Maine is an open records state, of course, but we will still need a warrant. And for that you'll need better grounds than simply, it may be relevant. Can't you give me a little more?"

I thought about it. "No," I said, "not right now, sir. I'll get back to you." I hung up. "Let's go find Angela Inglewood."

I opened the door, but she didn't get off the hood. When I stopped and stared at her, she said, "Am I just coming along for the ride, or are you going to tell me what we're doing? 'Cause I gotta tell you, partner, I'm beginning to get mighty pissed."

"Well," I said a little laboriously, "Copes won't talk to us, so we need to go and talk to Angela."

She sighed and climbed into the car beside me. "For what purpose, Stone?"

"Because," I said and started the engine, "we need to know who adopted Angela's son."

"Okay, even assuming that I knew how that would help us, she won't know who adopted her son."

"That's true." I nodded quite a lot. "That is true, theoretically, Dehan. But I have a feeling she might know how we can find out, without getting a court order in Maine. It's just a hunch for now, and something Cathy said. Just humor me for now, okay?"

I drove fast, a little too fast, along the Bruckner Expressway, and turned south at the Bruckner Interchange. I hit a hundred a couple of times, and a couple of times I hit a hundred and ten. After a while her silence got to me, and I said:

"If I tell you what I'm thinking, Dehan, you'll tell me I'm nuts and have nothing to go on. So I am trying to prove a couple of points before I reveal my brilliant deductions to you, see?"

"That is *not* how it works, Stone!"

"I know, I know, but bear with me."

"Why are you driving so fast?"

"Because, because, because, because . . ." I slowed, came off the I-295 onto East 177th, and went as fast as caution allowed for the mile or so till Pennyfield Avenue. Then I turned left into Chaffee and skidded to a halt outside Angela's house. I had the door open before I'd killed the engine, and ran along the path between the hedges to jump up the steps and hammer on her front door. I turned to Dehan. "Get the back!"

She wanted to argue, but she didn't. She pushed open the iron gate at the side of the house and went through. I hammered a bit more and rang on the bell, but there was no reply. Dehan reappeared.

"There is nothing back there. It's all locked up. She's not here."

I pulled out my cell and called Cathy.

"Yes, Detective . . ."

"Is Angela there with you, Cathy?"

"No. I was going to call you. I telephoned her after you left and said we needed to speak. I told her she needed to tell you about Sebastian Copes. She was terribly angry, called me all sorts of names."

"She's not at home. Any idea where she might have gone?"

"No, I mean, Guadalupe does all her shopping for her, so she won't be at the grocery store. But she may have gone anywhere, really . . ."

I thanked her and hung up. Dehan said, "What's going on, Stone? Did you know she wouldn't be here? Was that why you were speeding?"

"It was just a hunch. But I should have known."

I made a quick search, found Copes and Sanders' number, and called. A bright, merry voice answered, "Copes and Sanders Graphic Design! How may I direct your call?"

"Good morning, this is Saatchi Advertising, of London, and I would like to speak to Mr. Copes *muy pronto* because I am about to climb on a plane and I will not have a signal."

Fifteen seconds later Copes came on the line, trying to sound cheerful.

"Angus, is that you?"

I didn't even try to sound like my name was Angus. Instead I said, "Copes, I can do one of two things, I am going to let you decide which. I can get a court order to raid your office and your homes, with all the attended cop cars, flashing lights, sirens, and publicity, on the grounds that you have Angela Inglewood held hostage. Or I can come to your office right now, with three cruisers, sirens blaring and lights flashing, and march into your office claiming probable cause. Which do you recommend?"

"Detective Stone, what do you want?"

"I told you what I want, and I asked nicely. You didn't want to play softball, so now we're playing hardball. I have reason to believe that you have abducted Angela Inglewood."

His voice became shrill. "*That is ridiculous!*"

"Is it? Good. But before I let you off the hook, Copes, you'll have to explain to me what, exactly, makes it ridiculous. Now, if I have to apply for a warrant, I am going to put on a show that will make Spielberg look like Ingmar Bergman. If I have to come there now, I will bring at least three patrol cars with me, and they will all have their sirens wailing and their lights flashing, as promised. So I suggest that you do your civic duty and come and see me at the Forty-Third."

"Goddamn it! *Goddamn it!* I haven't got time for this!"

"Then make time, Copes, because believe me, you haven't got time for the other either."

"Fine, I'll be there in half an hour."

When I hung up, Dehan spread her hands and raised her shoulders. "Are you losing your *mind*? You think Copes has *abducted* her? Based on what?"

"I don't. But if my hunch is right, she could be seriously at risk."

"Angela? At risk? Who from?"

I gave my head a single shake. "If she's not dead already."

TEN

I'd put out a BOLO on Angela Inglewood and her car, which her sister had told me was a cream Volkswagen GTI. After that we'd made our way to the precinct, at a more sedate pace. When we got there Maria, on the desk, told us that Sebastian Copes had arrived and had been shown to interview room three. He wasn't happy and had called the coffee he'd been offered bat's piss. I didn't like his manners, but I couldn't argue with his assessment of the coffee.

We didn't stop for bat's piss but went straight to the interrogation room. He had an expression of elaborate incredulity on his face as he watched us come in and sit across from him at the table. Before either of us could say anything, he started shaking his head.

"I am sorry, was I the only one who heard, 'twenty minutes'? I mean, because I thought I said it very clearly, and I was here after twenty minutes and . . ."

Dehan sighed. "Shut up, Sebastian." He stopped dead, and his mouth sagged open. Dehan didn't stop. "This is a murder inquiry, and we haven't decided yet whether you are a suspect or not. If you're busy, so are we."

"*What? Me? A murder* suspect?"

"Quit bellyaching, let's get this done and maybe you can go home."

"*Maybe?*" He stared from me to Dehan and back again. "Do I need a lawyer?"

I shook my head. "No, not just yet, but the sooner you stop complaining, the quicker we can get this over with."

He pointed at Dehan like he was about to say something but remained silent. I fought back a smile and asked him my first question.

"When Angela went to see you that day, twenty years ago, when she resigned and told you your relationship was finished, exactly what reason did she give you? What did she tell you?"

"Are you telling me Angela has been murdered?"

"No, this is a murder inquiry, Mr. Copes, but Angela has not been murdered."

"Who then?"

Dehan cut in. "How about you stop asking questions and start answering ours, Sebastian? What did she tell you?"

He sagged back in his chair and rubbed his face with long, boney hands.

"*Jesus Christ!* I mean, it was *twenty years ago!*"

"You keep bullshitting and this is going to be a very long interview."

He threw his hands in the air. "Let me see if I can remember, *verbatim,* everything that was said *twenty years ago!* She came in. She'd been off sick for a week or something. I was expecting, fully expecting, that when she came back she was going to tell me that she would be mine. That she would marry me and we could be together. I was *so* excited. Impatient. And when she came in, and came into my office, and I looked at her face, I knew I had got it *badly* wrong.

"She looked at me with those blue, blue eyes, and that look . . ." He waved a hand, like he was polishing glass. "It said everything I needed to know. She sat and started crying, like *she* wanted sympathy from *me*."

I tried not to show my impatience. "What did she tell you?"

"That she and her husband had been talking—that was obviously the real reason she had taken the week off, to talk to that *plumber* or whatever he was—and they were going to try and save their marriage. Pathetic, emotionally stunted intellectual *dwarves*!

"She cried, I comforted her, like a schmuck, I begged her to reconsider. I mean . . ." He shrugged and spread his hands. "Why was she crying? I asked her, 'Honey, why are you crying, baby?' You know what she said? Go on, guess!"

I shook my head. "No."

"'Because I love you, I don't want to leave you, and I can't bear the thought of being without you!'" His voice became shrill, his eyes bulged, and he half stood. "*Well don't go! Don't leave! Stay here with me!* It is not rocket science! If it makes you happy to be with me, *stay with me*!"

He put his fingertips to his forehead and screwed up his eyes. "I mean, tell me! Please tell me if there is something wrong with my reasoning!"

"Mr. Copes . . ." He opened his eyes and stared at me. "You're going to have to calm down a little. So she told you she was leaving. What else did she tell you?"

"I told you, that she was going to try to make it work with that Neanderthal . . ."

"No." I shook my head. "What else did she tell you, Mr. Copes?"

He chewed his lip at me for a moment, then with a sudden jerk of his head turned to stare reproachfully at the wall.

"I don't know what you're talking about."

I leaned forward with my elbows on the table. "You don't know what I am talking about?" He didn't answer, just stared at the wall. "Mr. Copes, I think you're an intelligent man. You couldn't have achieved everything you have achieved if you were not intelligent. But I think you are too emotional to think clearly sometimes." He turned now to stare at me, and there was rage in his eyes. I pointed at his face. "There, right there, is what I am talking about. Your emotions flare up, you go crazy, and you don't think about the consequences of what you're saying or doing until it's too late."

I could see his chest rising and falling. His hands twitched a couple of times like he was about to get to his feet.

"How long," I said, "do you think it will take me to get a court order?"

I knew it was a question he could not answer, because he had no idea where we were in the investigation, or what we had managed to find out already. But it was something I wanted him to think about.

I leaned back and crossed my arms. "See, you have to consider the possibility that I already know the answer to what I am asking you." His eyes snapped onto mine. "So why would I ask anyway, you're wondering. Well, for a start, if you do become a suspect in my murder inquiry, I'd like to know how willing you are to tell the truth, how willing you are to lie, and what kind of things you might want to keep secret. Because this might all go to motive. So I would think very carefully before lying about something I can find out by applying to a friendly judge. Now, you want to do this again? What did she tell you?"

Disgust vied with contempt for dominance on his face. Disgust won.

"I guess that's just typical of cops, isn't it?"

"I guess it is. Now answer the question."

"*Fine!* She told me she was pregnant! I asked if I was the father, and she said of course I was. Her pathetic husband was impotent. So I begged her. I actually . . ." He gestured silently down at the floor with his upturned palm. "I *actually* got on my *knees* and *begged* her! Right there in the office. I begged her to marry me and allow me to raise the child as our child. Together. But she refused."

Dehan spoke for the first time in a while, frowning at Sebastian. "How was she going to explain the baby to her husband if he was impotent?"

He didn't look at her. His face was like stone. "You already know the answer to that."

"Tell me anyway."

"They had already been through that. He had thought it was his, they were rejoicing over having conceived *my* baby! And then his test results came through and he discovered that he was impotent!"

She was quiet for a moment. "So my question stands. If she wasn't going to leave him and marry you, what was the plan?"

He stared hard at the tabletop. He looked like he was trying to control his breathing, biting his lips. Finally he took a deep breath and spoke.

"She had decided to give it up for adoption."

She raised an eyebrow. "How did you feel about that?"

"What are you, a fucking psychiatrist now?" He made an absurd, mimicking voice. "'How did that make you feel?' It made me feel sick! And angry, and hurt! Like she was tearing out my guts and stamping on them! How do you think it made me fucking feel? You stupid . . ."

I cut him short. "Watch your mouth, Copes. That's the second time I've had to warn you."

He clamped it shut and looked at me with tears in his eyes. "It was a stupid question."

"Not so much, apparently. Did she tell you where she was going to have the baby?"

He hesitated then said, "No."

I waited. He didn't go on, so I said, "But you put a private detective on her."

"Yes."

"And when she went to the clinic to have the baby, he followed her there too, and found out where she was going to give the child up for adoption."

He nodded. "Yes, obviously, as you said, you knew all this already."

"Yeah, I knew it. But I need you to confirm the last part for me. I can get the court order, especially after this interview, but it would be easier if you told me. Easier for me, and for you."

He held my eye for a long time, then took a deep breath. "I went to the orphanage, I told them who I was, I offered to pay for a paternity test and they agreed, I demonstrated that I was financially more than viable as a father, and I demonstrated that the child would get the best care with me, with his father, and I took the child home with me."

"So, all these years, the child has been with you."

"Yes."

"What's his name?"

"Does it matter?"

"Yeah, it matters. What's his name?"

"Jonathan."

"Where is he now?" He stared at the wall and didn't answer. I repeated, "Where is he now?"

"That's quite enough, Detective. You've had your fun. If you have any further questions for me, you can address them to my attorney, Paul Hirschfield, at Wachtell, Lipton, Rosen and Katz. As of now, we are done here."

He stood. I said, "Has he been in touch with his mother?"

He made for the door. I stood and called after him. "Does he know who his mother is?"

He pulled open the door and turned to look at me. I said, "You wanted to know who got murdered." He hesitated. I said, "Chuck." His face registered nothing. I said, "Chuck Inglewood. The man Angela left you for."

He remained motionless for a long while, then shook his head. "This has nothing to do with me. You have brought all this madness into my life, but it has nothing to do with me. She gave me a son, twenty years ago, and she vanished. Leave us alone, or I'll see to it that you both lose your jobs."

"Does he know, Mr. Copes?"

His face went crimson, and he screamed at me, "*That's none of your goddamn business!*"

"Does he know?"

I could see the vein pulsing in the side of his head; his neck was corded. He struggled to slow his breathing. "No," he said at last. "No, he doesn't know who she is. He was never curious and never asked. He is happier this way."

"Is he?"

"That"—he bared his teeth and stabbed a finger at me—"that is none of your goddamn business! You stay away from my son!"

"I can't promise that, Mr. Copes. In fact, I would suggest that you bring your son in to talk to us as soon as you possibly can."

He waved his finger at me, licked his lips, swallowed, and waved his finger some more. "Just, *stay away*, you understand me? I can hurt you, I can make trouble for you." His voice broke, and tears formed in his eyes. "You stay away. From my family, you stay away."

He walked out, and the door swung closed behind him. I turned to look at Dehan. She was still sitting, half-turned in her chair, watching me. "Poor bastard," I said.

"You want to tell me what just happened? It's not fair, Stone, bringing me into an interrogation blind like that."

I went and sat in the chair Copes had just vacated. "Sorry."

"Sorry?"

"I didn't know, Dehan. It was just a hunch, and I played it."

"That was a pretty good hunch."

Her face said she wasn't sure whether to admire me or kick me. I lifted my shoulders.

"He was telling us he was crazy about her. You saw that yourself. You just have to look at the guy . . ." I gestured with my open hand at the closed door. "You just have to look at him to see that he is intensely emotional."

"But, Stone, how did you know she'd told him? Cathy, and *he*, both said that she had not!"

I sighed. "You remember I asked you if there was anything that struck you as odd in the way he spoke, or the things he said?"

"Yeah, and I said then what I would say now, you mean apart from everything?"

"Right, and I said that the fact she had turned up in person to tell him their relationship was over, that she was going to try to make it work with her husband, and that she had the *gall* to expect him to be grateful had struck me as odd."

"Uh-huh..."

"Well, there was something else, just before that, which I thought you might have picked up on. He said, and I'll try to remember it verbatim, 'She seduced me. Not the other way around. And then one fine day she comes into the office on Monday morning, after taking a week off sick, and...'"

I stopped. She waited. Then nodded. "That was all he said. I remember. And you prompted him."

"Exactly. It never really made sense to me that Angela would go there in person to break up, if she wasn't going to tell him she was pregnant. And when he said that 'and,' and stopped dead like that, I was pretty convinced he was about to say she'd told him, but stopped himself.

"It followed naturally that a man like him would not let it rest at that. He would hound her and pester her. And if he couldn't persuade her, if he knew she was going to give up the child for adoption, it was a no-brainer that he'd intervene and keep the kid. It was his child, after all."

She was quiet for a long time. "Why didn't I see that?"

I smiled. "Because you were focusing on Gore."

She nodded once, but then frowned at me.

"But, Stone, this doesn't actually change anything, because there is still no way I am buying that Copes killed Chuck. He may have had a theoretical motive twenty years ago, but keeping the kid settled it for him. Two years ago, he no longer had a motive. Hell, he didn't even know who Chuck was!"

"He didn't know the name."

"Just now, he didn't know he was dead, Stone!"

"Perhaps." I thought for a minute, sucking on my teeth.

"Would you accept that he is eccentric enough to have performed such a bizarre murder?"

"Yeah, I would agree with that. He is all kinds of batshit crazy. But he did not kill Chuck Inglewood."

I snorted a laugh. "I mean, I can understand you saying, 'I don't believe he did it,' or, 'I don't *think* he did it,' or even, 'I'm not *convinced* he did it.' But not good old Carmen Dehan. No, Little Grasshopper Carmen Dehan says, 'He didn't do it.'"

She regarded me under hooded eyes. "Shut up, wiseass." She stood and paced the room with her hands in her back pockets. "Besides, this guy's nerves are so out of control there is no way he could have cleaned up the way that killer did."

I nodded, and then nodded some more. "And therein, my dear Dehan, therein lies the mystery, and the answer to the mystery."

"Yeah? Is this another hunch, or do you care to enlighten me?"

"Nope, because I am not one hundred percent certain yet. I need a couple of things confirmed."

Her eyebrows crawled slowly up her forehead. "Are you telling me you know who dunnit and how dunnit?"

"I think so."

"Ha!"

"What do you mean, ha?"

"The hell you do!"

"I do."

"Prove it! Go on! Prove it! There is no way, *no way* you can know, in all this mess and confusion, how that murder was committed and by whom!"

"I do."

"Tell me."

"No."

"Ha! *Ha!*"

I reached over and took a sheet from her notepad. I scrawled a name on it, and a number, folded it in half, waved it at her, and put it in my wallet.

She harrumphed, then spread her hands in a gesture of helplessness. "Come on, Stone! This is stupid. We're cops! This is not a game! You have to tell me! I'll complain to the chief."

I stood and laughed softly in a way that I knew was both annoying and patronizing. "But first lunch, Ritoo Glasshopper. It has been a long morning. After lunch you can complain to the inspector."

She groaned and stood, muttering something about giving her patience.

ELEVEN

"I said," Dehan said, dangling a long piece of pepperoni pizza over her mouth, "Lord, give me patience, but don't give me strength! Because if you give me strength I'll tear his damned head off!"

"Nice."

She chewed on the half slice she had managed to fit in her mouth. "It was one of my mother's favorite expressions. To which my dad would always reply, 'Patience he gives to the Jews, so they can put up with crazy Catholics like you!' It was fun."

"Catholics . . ." I gazed out the window at the colliding streams of humanity steadily bobbing, weaving, and dodging each other along the sidewalks. "Anglicans, Methodists, Protestants . . ."

"What about them? Where'd you go, Stone? Come back." She was grinning and chewing. It made me smile.

"Nah, I was thinking about guilt. She must be feeling guilty. She's pretty religious, and it's a long chain of sins that have come back and bitten her in the ass."

"Angela?"

I grunted a nod. "First she conceived the child through adultery, then she abandoned it and gave it up for adoption, she lied to her husband . . ."

"You think she's gone to her minister?"

I shook my head. "She'd be too ashamed to face him."

"You think she's gone to look for her son? Stone, is this a priority? I don't see how it ties in. If you know who killed Chuck, and it wasn't Gore, you need to tell me."

"I don't *know*, Dehan, not for sure. I mean, I know, but I need to confirm a couple of things. What I do know is right there, as clear to you as it is to me: *All* the blood was on the bed, and on the floor around the bed. There was *no blood* on the wooden floor between the bed and the bathroom, but there *were* specks of blood in the grouting between the tiles and around the taps *in* the bathroom. All the blood—*all* the blood, Dehan—was on the bed, and a little in the bathroom . . ."

Her jaw sagged as realization dawned. "Holy sh . . . !"

I sat back. "But like I said, there are things I need to confirm."

"You think he had a lover! That's why he was on the bed!" She pointed at me, eyes wide. "That's why he was in that vulnerable position. His thighs exposed, his arms apart . . . Jesus, Stone! Why didn't I think of that?"

"Well," I said, "you just did."

"But you had to stick it right under my nose! It's so obvious! But . . ." She picked up a piece of pizza and her eyes darted up to the wall, across to the window, back to my face. She laid down the pizza again. "It affects the timing."

"Yes."

"Angela went out. Either his lover was waiting, or he called her."

"There was no such call on his phone."

"So she was a neighbor! Someone close enough to signal to. When Angela went out, she slipped in, and they went up to the bedroom. And of course that accounts for the absence of blood-stained clothes—she got undressed, but he didn't. She put her clothes to one side, maybe in the bathroom." She snapped her fingers. "They were playing a game. She was undressing him. She had the blade concealed. It wasn't a big blade, so maybe it was in her brassiere. His eyes are closed, she pulls out the blade and drives it deep into his thigh. Then she stabs him in the other, then his arms. She has blood on her hands, but not on the rest of her body. She hurries to the bathroom, quickly showers, and gets dressed. While she's doing that, he's bleeding out fast, but he desperately tries to call Angela, while his life is ebbing away. Man! She and Angela must have missed each other by seconds."

I watched her a moment while she thought, putting the pieces together in her mind. She frowned.

"That narrows the field right down, Stone. Somebody physically close enough to know when Angela had gone out, with a close enough relationship to . . ." Her face froze, her eyes went wide, and she slapped her forehead with the heel of her hand. "Son of a *bitch*! And you knew! You saw this from the start! No wonder you turn me on! Son of a *bitch*! It was Cathy!"

I drained my beer and smacked my lips. She frowned. "But why? What's her motive?"

I shrugged my eyebrows. "The motive for me was always the rape, but there may be more to it than that."

"Okay." She sat nodding for a while. "Cathy always felt for Chuck. He was just the kind of man Patrick wasn't. Patrick was distant, cold, academic, *uninvolved*." She pointed at me. "Remember when Angela left Chuck and moved in with them? He avoided her and Cathy, didn't want to know, retreated to his books. And Cathy, even though she supported her sister, felt for Chuck." She wagged the pointing finger. "And from that point on, she began to develop feelings for him. Compassion turned to love. And he, feeling betrayed by his wife, punished Angela and, in the process, healed his own bruised ego by having an affair with her sister! Man! It's textbook."

She leaned back in her chair, picked up her glass, and put it down again.

"The affair goes on for years, on and off, flaring up and dying down again. Then every time one of them feels injured or frustrated, the other is there to console them, and it is rekindled.

"But then, two years ago, the situation with Sadie and her friends becomes toxic. She is getting into drugs, she's becoming promiscuous, his feelings for her, which have always been unclish…"

"Displaced paternal."

"Exactly! Displaced paternal, become confused. Who knows if she even came on to him, Stone. From what we saw on her phone, she was getting pretty crazy. Either way, he finds he is becoming jealous of her sexual adventures. Did he rape her? Was it somebody else? We'll never know, and it doesn't really matter; what matters is that Cathy believed he did. Maybe Sadie accused him; maybe she hinted, as a way to get back at him for what he did to Gore. And right there is Cathy's motive. Stone, you are a genius."

I sighed. "Well, the credit must go to you, kiddo, if nothing else, for the way you told it. It is very compelling. I do wonder, though, why there was no blood on her body. His thighs would have been pumping out a lot of blood."

"Not impossible, Stone. Leave the knife in and smother the wound with the duvet; when the first gush is over, go for the other thigh. By the time she gets to his arms, it's no longer a spray but an ooze."

I sucked my teeth. "Hmmm, perhaps. The problem remains, how do we prove it?" I drummed my hands on the table. "We should really talk to Angela's son."

Dehan raised an eyebrow at me. "You're fixated on that, Stone. I don't see the relevance. How does he tie into this?"

And as she asked it the last pieces began to fall into place in my mind.

"Goddamn it!" I said and stood, snatching my wallet from my coat. "Genius? I'm a damn idiot!"

I threw a fistful of money on the table and made for the door, with Dehan scrambling to catch up. "Why? What happened?"

"Don't talk." I pushed out of the restaurant and made for the car. Then stopped, with my hand on the handle, and pointed at Dehan. "Sorry. For a moment. Don't talk. Listen: call Cathy. Find out where she is. Wherever she is, tell her to stay there, we are sending a car for her. Then, send a car for her and have it take her to the station house. We hold her as a material witness."

"*What?* To what? We can't prove any of this yet, Stone. It's just a theory!"

"Don't argue! Then, have the BOLO on Angela and her car put out in Maine, and in particular Portland! Get in the car!"

She climbed in, dialing. "You'd better tell me what the hell is going on, Stone."

"I will, just as soon as I know . . ."

I fired up the engine. She said, "There's no reply. I'll try the house."

She hung up, dialed, and started talking as I pulled away. "Yeah, Dr. Byrne, this is Detective Dehan of the . . . Exactly. Listen, I need to talk to your wife . . . She's not there? You don't know . . . Fine, when she gets in will you have her call me at this number, immediately. It is very urgent . . . Yeah, you too."

She hung up and started dialing again, muttering, "Son of a bitch couldn't care less. Didn't even ask . . . Yeah, this is Detective Carmen Dehan . . ."

I zoned out, thinking about Cathy, Angela, and Sebastian Copes; and Angela and Sebastian's son, Cathy's nephew; and who knew what about whom.

It was a three-hundred-mile, four-and-three-quarter-hour journey from the Bronx to Portland, in Maine, practically all of it on the I-95. It was four and three-quarter hours if you stuck to the speed limit, but I had no intention of sticking to the speed limit. I am of the view that a one-hundred-mile journey along an American interstate highway should take one hour. So it was a little after three hours later that we entered Cumberland County in Maine. Along the way, Dehan had found Mary Finch's telephone number and found that she was at work, at the Cressy Home for Abandoned Children. Mary Finch had been Angela and Cathy's old friend from Portland, who had helped with the adoption.

So we continued along the Maine Turnpike, took exit 46, and turned west onto Skyway Drive. After that we followed County Road back on ourselves for three miles till we came to a remote, country intersection and turned onto South Street, leading, through abundant trees and greenery, to the orphanage.

It was a Georgian manor house, set in its own grounds, on the outskirts of the town of Gorham. We pulled in through the large iron gates and parked the Jag outside the front door, at the foot of a sweep of five broad stone steps that supported two Greco-Roman pillars which in turn held a Palladian pediment. Flanking this were Palladian arched windows.

Inside, through the large, double wooden doors, the hall was a gloomy, hushed haven of shadows and whispers, populated by mahogany wall panels and a large, sober mahogany staircase, carpeted in burgundy. The hall itself had a checkerboard floor and a long, mahogany desk along the right-hand wall. Our heels tapped and echoed above our heads as we made for the reception, and a steely-haired woman in a blue suit watched us, smiling, and waited.

I produced my badge, smiled back, and showed it to her.

"I'm Detective Stone of the New York Police Department. We are here with the knowledge and consent of the Gorham PD. You can call them if you need . . ."

"They already called us, Detective Stone. You want to talk to Mary?"

"Yes, please. She's expecting us."

"I'll just call her and let her know you're here."

Two minutes later we heard a heavy tread on the wooden stairs, and a woman who had once been pretty, petite, and mischievous, but had since sold her soul to Public Services, hurried down the stairs holding the banisters for support. She had broad hips and powerful legs, and a smile that wanted to be naughty but had forgotten how. She started speaking as she reached the bottom of the stairs.

"Detective Stone, Detective Dehan, I am just plain Mary Finch. I am delighted to meet you. How can we be of help to you at Cressy?"

We shook hands and Dehan asked, "Is there somewhere we can talk in private?"

"Of course." She pointed to a door in the wall opposite the reception desk. "We can go in the library." She led the way, talking as she strutted. "We try to encourage the children to read as much as possible, but they are all in class at the moment."

She seized the handle and pushed through, standing back to let Dehan and me in. It was a long, oblong room lined with heavy wooden bookcases made of a highly polished dark red wood. The far wall was a procession of Palladian arched windows intersected by narrow bookcases and desks with reading lamps. Dehan looked around with a quizzical smile. "The kids read here?"

Mary Finch smiled and nodded. "They love it. It reminds them of Harry Potter." She became conspiratorial. "And we've found, if you don't tell children they are supposed to have zero attention span and a limited vocabulary, and think stupid kids are smart and smart kids are stupid, they just behave like normal, healthy, bright children."

"Well, whadd'ya know!"

"We are privately funded, Detective Dehan, and we do not subscribe to the dumbing down ethos that has plagued our educational system for the last forty years. The children who get to stay here and are not adopted benefit from a world-class education."

She sat at one of the tables by one of the arched windows. Half her face was caught in a hazy glow of light. The other half was in shadow. She looked at us in turn and repeated her earlier question. "Now, how can we help you?"

We sat opposite her, and after a moment's thought I shook my head. "Not 'we,' Ms. Finch."

"I am a Miss, not a Ms., and you can call me Mary, please."

"Okay, Mary, not 'we,' but you. Let me make this clear. We have no jurisdiction here, so you can tell us to go to hell anytime you like. But we *are* here with the consent of the Gorham PD, and they have offered their help should we need it."

"That sounds like a threat, or at least a warning. Are you sure you need to go down that route? So far I have said I am willing to help."

"No, it's not a threat at all." I followed that up with a smile. "Nor a warning. I just want to make you aware of the situation. You see, we are interested in a friend of yours."

"Of mine?"

"Yes, her husband was murdered a couple of years ago, and we are investigating his death. Her name is Angela Inglewood."

"Angie . . . !"

"Yes."

Her face became serious. "What do you want to know about her?"

"Like I said, Mary, we have no jurisdiction here. We can and will seek a judicial order if necessary, but things have taken an unexpected turn, and lives could be at stake." I sensed rather than saw Dehan's eyebrows twitch but ignored them and went on. "So this is a matter of urgency."

She nodded with a touch of irritation. "Okay, I understand that, Detective. What do you want to know?"

I held up one finger. "Two things. One, I want to know where she is."

"What makes you think I would know?"

I played a powerful hunch that had been eating at me since before lunch and said, "Because she came to see you today." I watched her face. Her jaw sagged a little, but she didn't say anything. I raised a second finger and went on, "And two, I need to know whether she knows what happened to her child after she left him here to be adopted."

"Let me take these in turn," she said, with some asperity. "In the first place, no, she certainly does *not* know what happened to her child after she left him for adoption. That information is confidential, and such a disclosure would be highly irregular."

"She is your friend," I insisted.

"Friend or no friend, Detective, that information is confidential." She paused. "And second of all, I have absolutely no idea where Angela is."

I nodded and sighed then glanced at Dehan. "I guess we've wasted our time and come here for nothing, then."

Mary spread her hands and gave a self-satisfied little shrug. "I'm afraid so. Rules is rules."

"Except that"—I sighed noisily and flopped back in my chair—"I don't believe you." Her face went rigid, and I slowly shook my head at her. "You see, I know that Angela *needs* to know what happened to her son. And the only way she can find out is through you. So she *has* been in touch with you. And the fact that you have lied about her contacting you, or coming to see you, tells me you, as her friend, have given her the information she was after. Now, here's the thing: if you don't give *us* the information *we* need, today, right now, at least one person will probably be killed." I pointed at her. "And it will be your fault."

I paused, giving that time to sink in. Then added, "I know that Angela has been here, Mary. I know that for a fact. She was just one or two hours ahead of us. She was here, and she asked you what happened to her son. And you told her that he had been taken by Sebastian Copes, his biological father."

I saw her cheeks color and her pupils contract. It was as clear as a confession, and it confirmed my hunch.

"How long ago was she here, Mary?"

She drew breath. For a moment her eyes were hard. Then she sagged and let the breath out through puffed cheeks.

"Just over an hour ago. She wanted to know if Sebastian had adopted Jonathan. I told her I couldn't give her that information, but she was practically hysterical. So in the end I told her he had."

"Did she tell you how she came to suspect he had adopted

him in the first place?" She hesitated. I pressed her, "Come on, Mary. This is important. Did Chuck tell her?"

I sensed Dehan's eyes burning holes in my head, but Mary was nodding. "Yes, she said Chuck had told her shortly before he died, and she had not wanted to believe it."

"Did she tell you how Chuck found out?"

"No." She shook her head. "I asked her, but she wouldn't tell me. She asked if I had any idea of John, her son's, current whereabouts. I told her I had no idea and she left, in great distress. I asked her to see a doctor, or her minister, or at least to tell me what was upsetting her. But she wouldn't, and she drove away."

Dehan wasn't frowning, she was scowling. "And you thought it was smart to lie to us about this?"

Mary's cheeks flushed. "As your partner said, Angela has been a friend for over thirty years. And quite honestly, she already had the information and she was in such a state of distress. And . . ." She gave a helpless shrug. "I just don't see that this can have anything to do with Chuck's murder. It all happened so many years ago! It seems to me absurd to make such a connection."

I leaned forward and fixed her with my eyes. "That, Mary, is not a decision for you to make. Let's just hope it's not too late."

"Too late . . . ?"

We stood, and Mary followed us to the library door, clenching her hands over her womb. I pulled the door open, paused, and frowned.

"Tell me something. How do you name the kids that get left here? I figure most of them don't have names when they're dropped off, right?"

She looked surprised.

"No, very rarely. At most they might have a first name or a nickname. But usually they are unnamed, and the staff get together and put forward a few names they think fit the child. Then we take a vote."

"What about surnames? They must need surnames for paperwork, insurance . . ."

"Well, most often the birth parents don't want the child to have *their* surname, for all sorts of obvious reasons. So we use a number of different options, depending on the case. Often we'll give the child the name of the town where he or she was born, you know, if it fits. Then, when they're adopted, they take their adoptive parents' surname."

"And Jonathan?"

She frowned. "Well, he was claimed by his father just hours after he was left here, and collected very shortly after that, so it didn't really arise."

"Sure."

I nodded, and we thanked her and left.

Outside, Dehan stood in the afternoon sun as I unlocked the car door, and said, "Somebody might get murdered if she didn't tell you whether Angela had been here?"

I nodded. "One person has been murdered already."

She didn't answer for a moment. Then, "You knew Angela needed to know whether her son had been adopted by Sebastian Copes? You knew Chuck had told her? Stone, what the hell is going on in your head?"

"Not now, Dehan. I need to think. We need to get back to New York fast, and you need to locate Cathy."

I climbed in, and she climbed in after me, scowling and reaching for her phone. I pulled out of the orphanage and accelerated fast through the village toward South Street. As we passed through the town, Dehan did a double take, flopped her head back against the seat, and closed her eyes. I heard her mutter, "Jesus!"

I did seventy down County Road while Dehan dialed and tried Cathy again. There was still no response. So she called Patrick Byrne and put him on speaker.

"Dr. Byrne, this is Detective Dehan again."

"Yes, I know who you are, Detective, and no, I still have no idea where my wife is. She is an adult woman who has complete freedom to do as she pleases with her life. If she is not answering her telephone, it is probably because she does not want to speak to you. A strategy I may start to adopt myself! Good day!"

She stared at the phone a minute and her nostrils dilated. "Well, that told me."

At the Congress Street intersection I made the Jag skid round the corner, which is not easy to do, and with screaming tires I roared down Skyway Drive and hit a hundred on the service road to join the Maine Turnpike.

As we crossed the Saco River, with Biddeford and Saco on our left, Dehan pulled out her cell again and dialed a number. Again she put it on speaker, and after a couple of rings I recognized Sebastian Copes' voice. It sounded haggard and drained.

"Yes?"

"Mr. Copes, this is Detective Dehan."

"I know. What do you want? I thought I told you to communicate with my lawyer."

"Yeah, you did. But I'm afraid there is no time for that now. I need to know if you've seen your son."

There was a long silence. "No."

"When was the last time you did see him?"

A loud sigh. "He's an adult," he said, in a strange echo of what Patrick Byrne had said. "He comes and goes . . . I don't know, a couple of weeks maybe. Perhaps a little more. Why are you looking for him? You have no right . . ."

"We're not looking for him, Mr. Copes, but Angela Inglewood is, and we need to know why. If you contact him, or he contacts you, will you please let us know? You need to bring him to the station, urgently."

There was a long silence, then, "Should I be worried, Detective?"

She looked at me. I glanced back and shrugged my shoulders. I was pretty sure it was too late for that. She sighed.

"Maybe you should make an effort to contact him and see if he is okay, Mr. Copes. Just to be sure."

"To be sure of *what*?"

She hesitated. "That he's okay." She hung up and looked at me. "Are you sure about this?"

I shook my head. "No. Not yet." Then, reluctantly, "Yes. Yes, I am pretty sure."

"I'm not seeing the connection, Stone."

"It's there."

We got back to the Bronx at five p.m. and I headed straight for the Barnabas. We left the Jag in the parking lot, ran for the main entrance, and dodged through the crowds to the elevators. It took an eternity for one to arrive, and when it had arrived it took another eternity to get us to Gore's floor.

I'm not sure what I was expecting to find when I got there, but I know I was expecting to find something, someone—Gore. But what we actually found when we pushed through the door into his room was an empty bed.

"He's dead." Dehan stared at me. "He's dead . . ."

I stepped out and went to the desk, where I showed the pretty girl behind it my badge and said, "Where is the patient who was in that room?"

She smiled nicely and said, "What was their name?"

"He didn't have a name. He had no ID. His nickname was Gore. He had AIDS."

"Yes, I know who you're talking about . . ." Her eyes strayed over the computer screen and then over some forms clipped to a board.

"He went home."

"That's impossible. He was in a coma, and he had no home."

She nodded, still looking at her clipboard. "Doctors determined it was terminal, matter of days, possibly hours. His mother came in and took him home."

"His mother?"

She looked at me, like it was odd I should find that odd. "Yes, Detective. His mother. She checked him out and then took him home."

"How long ago?"

She checked again and glanced at the clock. "Just over an hour ago."

Dehan snapped, "He had no ID, how can you be sure it was his mother?"

The girl screwed up her face. "Because people don't normally go around kidnapping terminally ill AIDS patients, Detective. She identified him as her son, signed his release papers, and took him away."

I said, "Was it Angela Inglewood?"

She thrust the clipboard across the desk.

"That's what it says here."

TWELVE

We took the stairs down because they were faster than the elevators. As we burst through the fire door and strode across the lobby toward the doors, Dehan was shaking her head.

"What the hell is she doing, Stone? This is her son, but does she believe he killed her husband?"

"I don't know, Dehan," I said. "She needs to tell us that, but two gets you twenty she does not believe he killed Chuck."

"You think she knows it was Cathy? How could she know that? Unless..."

We clambered into the car. I turned the key, the engine roared, and I pulled out of the lot.

"Unless," she went on, "we put it together, Stone. When they rowed, maybe she put it together too. Cathy called her to tell her what Patrick had said, that she should tell us about Copes. Cathy said she got mad. Maybe Cathy got mad too. Maybe something Cathy said made Angela realize that she and Chuck had been lovers. Hell, if they were at it on and off for twenty years, she had to have suspected something, right? But this family seem to be masters at denial. She may have simply ignored it until now..."

"That's a lot of speculation, Dehan."

"Yeah, Stone, but it's all we got. And it is *not* speculation that Angela went to the orphanage to pump Mary Finch, and it is *not* speculation that she went and took Gore from the hospital."

We took the Bronx and Pelham Parkway as far as the New England Thruway, then turned south on the Bruckner Expressway and floored the pedal, hitting a hundred and twenty miles per hour as far as the Schneider Sampson Square. There I peeled off onto the I-295 toward the Throgs Neck Bridge, and came off just before, onto East 177th, making the rubber burn on my tires. Then it was left on Pennyfield and another screeching left into Chaffee.

Dehan had the door open before I hit the brakes. I killed the engine and followed her at a run, down the path between the hedges to the front door. She hammered and rang the bell.

I pulled my piece and said, "No time for that. Stand back."

I blew out the lock and kicked in the door, shouting, "*NYPD! Angela! Angela Inglewood! This is the NYPD!*"

But even as I was shouting, Dehan was shaking her head. "Stone, Stone! They're not here. *Shit!*" She slapped her forehead. "How could I be so stupid! Don't you see? It wasn't Angela! It was Cathy! Cathy checked him out!"

I had one foot on the stairs to go up to the bedrooms. I stopped and stared at her.

"Cathy? Why . . . ?"

"Because! Stone! It was Gore who raped Sadie! Cathy thought it was Chuck, and that's why she killed him. But when Cathy phoned Angela they rowed, right?"

I frowned. "Yes . . ."

"Cathy told us, like I said before, that Angela was furious."

"What are you driving at, Dehan?"

"Hell, Stone! Angela must have told Cathy not only what Chuck had told her about Gore, but also that he had AIDS! She must have realized then that Chuck's aggression toward Gore was not sexual jealousy over Sadie, it wasn't that he was attracted to Sadie himself, but simply a kind of displaced paternal protection toward her; and anger at Gore because he was Sadie's first cousin, and he was coming on to her! This was some sick game of Gore's, and Cathy must have realized that. Then, when Angela told her he had AIDS, she must have realized that it was him, and not Chuck, who had raped and infected her daughter!" We stared at each other a moment and she repeated, with emphasis, "They are not here, Stone! They are at Cathy's!"

I hesitated, then turned and ran up the stairs. Dehan followed, calling after me, "Stone! We can't waste time! We have to get to Cathy!"

I was on a broad landing with white banisters and wall-to-wall burgundy carpet. Four white doors faced me, one at the far end on my right, which stood half-open onto a bathroom. A second, immediately to my left, also stood open, onto a small bedroom which was cluttered with furniture and bags of clothes, obviously a storeroom. Two more stood closed in front of me.

I stepped forward and opened the second door on my left. It was empty: a guest room with a window overlooking Chaffee Avenue. I closed it and moved to the next, gripped the handle, turned, and went in.

The window was slightly open and lace curtains were wafting gently in the breeze. There was a king-size bed between the door and the window. Lying on the bed was Gore. He was dressed in jeans and a sweatshirt, but his sneakers had been removed. His mouth was slightly open. His skin was very pale, and his hands were resting gently on his belly.

Cathy was sitting in a chair on the far side of the bed. Her eyes were fixed on Gore, staring. Her hands were resting in her lap. Her expression was impassive, like his.

They were both dead.

Gore had a neat incision in the side of his neck. There was a large, dark stain on the duvet and the pillow, but he had not bled much. In his condition death had come quickly, and his heart, weakened already, had soon stopped pumping.

At first there was no obvious sign of what had killed Cathy.

She was sitting at a slight angle with the bright glare of the window behind her. In death, as in life, her skin was very pale, but where the lace curtains had wafted up and touched the back of her neck, they had come away red, stained with blood.

I moved around the foot of the bed and stood behind her. There I saw the neat cut, just at the base of her skull, where a very sharp knife had been slipped between her vertebrae. Death must have been instantaneous.

Dehan came beside me.

"I am struggling to keep up. What the hell has happened here?" She leaned forward and squinted at the wound. "A scalpel?"

"Could be, or an old-fashioned barber's razor. Even something homemade."

Her eyes traveled around the room while she thought.

"She collected him from the hospital..."

"On her own?"

She hesitated, like the question was unexpected. "I guess the hospital staff helped her. They must have brought him in an ambulance..."

"To Angela's house."

"Yeah." She frowned. "Why to Angela's house?" She made a face like she'd thought of something and figured maybe it was reasonable. "Because of her husband," she said. "With Patrick there, she can't take him to her own place. So she brings him here. Maybe she knew Angela was going to be away..."

She rubbed her face with her two hands. "Stone? Run through this with me, will you?" She held up one finger. "Chuck told Angela that Sebastian Copes had adopted their son, or at least taken him home with him. We don't know how he found out, but, like I said before, if he found out shortly before he was killed, it's a safe bet he knew it was Gore and that was why he was so mad at Gore for coming on to Sadie. Am I making sense so far?"

I nodded. "Eminent sense."

"So, just before he dies, Chuck tells Angela what he has found out. What prompts him to tell her, we don't know. She chooses either not to believe it, or to ignore it..."

I leaned against the wall and crossed my arms. "Again, as you said before, the impression we got from both of the sisters from the start was that they were both in denial about Sadie and Chuck. My feeling is, that's how they deal with most problems: ignore them until either they go away or it's too late."

"Right. Now, suddenly, as we start this investigation, Angela decides to act on what Chuck told her. What made her do that?"

"Apparently, the fact that Patrick decided we should know about her affair with Sebastian Copes."

"Because..."

I shrugged. "Because, if we started investigating Sebastian Copes, we must sooner or later..."

She interrupted me. "We must sooner or later hit on the fact that Gore was her son. So she had to either confirm or disprove that before we did. But the problem I'm having, Stone, is why is this an issue for her? Why does she not want us to know about her son?"

"Well..."

She waved a hand at me. "I know what you're going to say. Stay focused on what is relevant and stay on task. Okay, so, we are *assuming* Angela told Cathy that Gore was her son and he had AIDS. This, as we already said, is a bombshell for Cathy, who now realizes she murdered Chuck, the man she loved, without reason. So she decides to kill Gore..."

"But..."

She shook a finger at me. "No, wait, while Angela is in Portland, Cathy arranges, either with or without her sister's knowledge, to go and collect Gore and bring him here."

"How does she know that Angela's gone to Portland?"

"Because as soon as Cathy makes her decision to kill Gore, she sues for peace with Angela."

I smiled. "Sues for peace?"

"Yeah. Sues for peace. Listen, you told Angela that Gore was in the hospital, probably with AIDS, and Angela told Cathy. When Cathy heard that, and the awful truth dawned on her that she had murdered the man she loved for no reason, she decided to kill Gore. In that instant she also decided to make peace with Angela, because she was going to use her."

"Okay, so, according to that theory, posing as Angela, she goes to the hospital and brings him here . . ." I shook my head again. "Intending to do what? Kill him in her sister's house? What for?"

"To punish Angela? Because if Angela had not had her affair in the first place, none of this would have happened?"

I grunted. "That's a stretch, Dehan. Also, there is one small detail you seem to be overlooking." I pointed at Cathy's corpse sitting in the chair. "Cathy is dead, and she and Gore appear to have been killed with the same weapon, presumably by the same person." I sighed. "We'd better call this in."

While I did that, she stood staring at the two corpses. When I'd hung up, she said, "We need to find out where Sebastian Copes was today."

"I agree."

She kept talking, as though she hadn't heard me. "She wants to punish the people who destroyed her happiness and, in her mind at least, made her kill the man she loved. She is not going to be satisfied by simply killing a guy who is, for all intents and purposes, already dead." Now she raised her eyes to look at me. "She wants to spread it about a bit. So while Angela is in Portland she brings Gore here and kills him, so that Angela will walk in and find him here, dead.

"But that is not enough. Because, let's face it, Angela has lived without her son for years, and had in any case already given him up. Sure, it will hurt her, but not enough. The one person whom she can *really* hurt, and who was also partly responsible for her pain, is Sebastian Copes. So she calls him, tells him to come over, she has something to show him. And when he arrives she's sitting here, with Gore dead on the bed."

She paused again. Her eyes went back to Gore.

"She probably left the weapon on the bed, or on the bedside table. Copes simply picked it up and killed her. His left palm print will be all over her forehead."

"What about Angela?"

"She got home, found the bodies, panicked, and fled."

"Why'd she panic? Why not just call us? And where'd she run to?"

"Maybe she didn't run. Copes is pretty much on the top line at the best of times. He was pretty crazy about her. Maybe Angela got here before him. If he found them both here, maybe he killed Cathy and took Angela."

As she was saying it she was pulling her phone from her jacket. I could hear the muted *burr* of its ringing and at the same time the distant wail of approaching sirens. Dehan had the phone to her ear, watching me. She shook her head.

"It went to his answering service."

"Call the company."

I said it, but she was already doing it.

I looked out the window and saw the two patrol cars pull up outside with their lights flashing in the fading afternoon, beating a flickering tattoo on the wall of the house opposite. Not far behind them was the ME's car, and just behind that was the crime scene team in their van. They clustered around the gate, looking strangely like flies gathering on a corpse, and I pushed myself off the sill and made my way down to talk to Frank and Joe. Dehan came behind me, talking on the phone.

". . . I need to talk to him urgently . . . What time did he go out? . . . No, I'm getting no reply from his cell. Listen, you need to tell him that we have found his son and it's a matter of the utmost urgency that he get in touch with us . . ."

There was a scrum of uniforms and guys in white plastic suits in the front yard and spilling into the hall. The crime scene guys were carrying metal cases of equipment, tripods, and cameras. Joe was with them, inspecting the damage I'd done to the lock, and

Frank was standing in the middle of the floor, watching us descend.

I called out to Joe and pointed at the lock. "That was me. We were in a hurry. The bodies are upstairs, in the master bedroom." To Frank I said, "I know it's impossible, but it would be useful to know who died first."

He snorted as he started to climb the steps. "What was Nero Wolfe's favorite saying? 'Pfui, sir! Are you a dunce, or do you take me for one?'"

We joined Joe at the door as his boys filed past us and began to climb heavily after Frank, lugging their equipment with them. Dehan spoke first.

"The woman in the chair, upstairs. We figure she was stabbed with a sharp blade from behind, into the back of her neck. It's probable the killer held her forehead with his left palm when he did it." She demonstrated the action as she said it.

Joe glanced at her and nodded. "Prints from the forehead. Got it."

I said, "How about those sheets, Joe?"

"Yeah, that guy, he was stabbed to death, right?"

"Yeah, on the bed."

"Well, in the end we were able to get a sufficient sample from behind the tap, and the blood in the bathroom matches the blood on the sheet. So we can say conclusively that the blood in the bath was Chuck Inglewood's. Whether it was from the murder, or whether he fell in the bath or cut himself shaving, is impossible to tell. However, it is his blood."

I nodded. "But you were unable to find any on the wooden floor of the bedroom, between the bed and the bathroom."

"Not a drop. However, there was the interesting fact that the bedroom floor had been thoroughly cleaned. On close inspection, compared with the rest of the house and in particular the rest of the bedroom, that wooden floor was spotless."

"So somebody had taken the trouble to mop the bedroom floor."

"It sure looks that way. So the chances are there *were* traces of blood from the bed to the bathroom, but they were then mopped up."

Dehan was frowning hard. "But that completely screws the time frame."

Joe laughed. "Sorry 'bout that, Detective Dehan! What it does suggest is that the killer had a shower and then cleaned the floor in the bedroom and the bathroom. I don't know how long that would take without actually putting it to the test, but I'd say you're looking at a minimum of ten minutes. More like fifteen."

I nodded. "That's cutting it pretty tight." Then I walked to the bottom of the stairs and called up, "Hey Frank!"

He peered over the banisters. "I'm working."

"How long did Chuck Inglewood take to bleed out? Deep cuts into the basilica vein and the brachial artery, on both arms, and then deep into the inside thighs, femoral artery, the femoral vein, and the saphenous . . ."

He interrupted me. "I haven't got all day, and neither have you. It depends whether he is cut first in the thigh or first in the underarms. Either way he is not going to last more than five minutes, could be as little as one."

Dehan rubbed her face vigorously with both hands. "Man!" she said. "How does that work?"

I looked back at Joe. "And what about the sheets? The rest I had pretty much fathomed, but I need you to confirm the sheets for me."

He raised an eyebrow. "Fathomed? Confirm?"

I could feel Dehan glaring at me. I tried to ignore her and nodded at Joe. "Yeah, have you got a result on the sheets yet?"

"I would have, John." He shrugged and gestured toward the bedroom upstairs. "Give me a couple of hours or three."

THIRTEEN

I let him go, and we moved out into the front yard, followed the garden path through hedges to the sidewalk, and gazed up at the darkening sky.

"What is it with the sheets?"

I lowered my eyes. Her face was a grainy blur in the dusk. A cool breeze moved in from the creek, making the pines and the bulrushes whisper. It pulled a few strands of hair across her face, and she fingered them away.

"I asked him to analyze the blood . . ."

Her phone rang. She looked at the screen and said, "Hang on," and then into the phone, "Yeah, Dehan."

She listened a moment, then her gaze fixed on me like I'd said something. "Okay, got it. Thanks." To me she said, "East Hampton PD have spotted Angela's car."

"East Hampton?"

"Yeah, in Springs. On Parson Place by . . ." She fought to remain deadpan. "By Pussys Pond."

I rolled my eyes. "Come on, Mrs. Stone, let's go."

We took the Throgs Neck Bridge as night fell, and beyond the bizarre stage set of the long road, plunging through the blackness above the East River, small lights like distant stars winked and glinted like distant ice.

On the other side, we skimmed the shore of Little Neck Bay and turned east at Alley Pond Park onto the 495. After that it was ninety miles of pretty much straight road through sprawling, leafy suburbs and occasional dense, black woodlands.

We finally reached Springs at ten p.m. It was the kind of place Tolkien would have had twenty-first-century suburban elves living. You could barely see the houses for the trees, but you just knew that every house had a pool, a lawn, and a drinks cabinet, and every dinner party was preceded by lembas and dry martinis.

Parson Place was a short road with a small scattering of houses separated by well-tended lawns and dotted with trees that were impossible to identify in the darkness. On the left there was a building set back with a gravel parking lot. One car sat in it, a cream Volkswagen GTI.

I pulled in beside it, got out, and played my flashlight over the license plate. It was Angela's car. Dehan came and stood beside me, and we scanned the area. It was very quiet. Only the soft breeze in the young leaves and the lapping of the pond disturbed the dark silence. Dehan's voice was dry when she said, "So we found the car."

I tried the doors and the trunk but it was locked. "We don't know of any connection between the Inglewoods or the Byrneses and Long Island."

"No."

I pulled my cell and called the East Hampton PD. A sleepy voice answered.

"Yeah, this is Detective John Stone of the Forty-Third Precinct."

"How can I help you, Detective?"

"We put out a BOLO earlier on a cream Volkswagen GTI..."

"I remember. I think we found that for you, didn't we?"

There was a smile in his voice, and I returned it. "You sure did, and we're at the car right now, in Springs. We're very grateful."

"Glad we could help."

"I'm just wondering if you could help us a little more."

"Glad to if we can."

"It's a little delicate. This is part of a homicide investigation . . ."

"Don't get much of that round here."

"Yeah, it's not the Bronx. We're keen to talk to a man, I'm not sure, but he might be a resident here in Springs."

"What's the name?"

"Copes . . ."

"Sebastian? Sebastian Copes?"

"That's the man."

"Sure, they've had property in Springs for three generations, maybe more. His granddaddy used to flip me a dollar for cleaning his car." His voice became skeptical. "He's eccentric all right, but I'd be surprised if he's involved in anything illegal, Detective."

"He has a house here in Springs? Can you give me the address?"

There was a momentary silence and a rustle of papers. "You're at Parson Place right now?"

"Yeah."

"Well, I'll tell you. You continue on up Springs Fireplace Road for another seven hundred yards, you're gonna come to Talmage Farm Lane, where you're gonna make a sharp right. You follow that road for, oh, two hundred and fifty yards? You gonna come to a big, wooden gate, and that is the Copeses' house. Has been for a hundred years or more."

"Thanks, that's very helpful. Much obliged."

I hung up and smiled at Dehan. She shrugged. "Have you developed second sight? Were you abducted by aliens and they gave you superpowers?"

"No." I pointed north. "Seven hundred yards up Fireplace Road." I returned to the car and opened the door. "It was just a pretty safe guess, Dehan. We know of no connection between the

Byrneses or the Inglewoods and Long Island. But Copes told us he had a house in the country."

"He did? When?"

I climbed in, and she climbed in next to me. "When he was telling us everything he had offered Angela. Copes is not at his office, Angela's car is here, safe bet that his country house is in Springs."

She slammed her door. "I wish you at least sounded smug. Then I could legitimately resent you."

I pulled away and turned onto Springs Fireplace Road.

"Don't be sensitive, Dehan. It's not that you're slow. It's just that I am really, really smart, and you seem slow by comparison."

The punch on my shoulder hurt, but I smiled complacently, like it didn't.

There were no streetlamps and there was no moon, so we almost missed the turning on our right because it was shielded by dense trees and was not a road as such, but more like a broad dirt track. I had to brake and reverse, and then turn down into the woodland. There was space for only one car, and though the road surface was not pitted, I advanced slowly along the track.

After a couple of minutes we came to an intersection, with a road on the left that was lost among trees, and a large, wooden gate on the right. I put the Jag in neutral, and we climbed out to have a look.

Beyond the gate there was a broad, irregular yard that looked like it was asphalted. There was a barn or an outhouse on the left with a slate roof, and another on the right with the big, green doors slightly open. Nothing was visible inside except impenetrable shadows.

About fifty paces away there was a house. A single bulb in a shade shone over the front door. From where we were standing it looked like an old redbrick farmhouse, not elegant, but substantial and probably comfortable. The white-painted sash windows glowed faintly in the starlight. Two cars were parked outside: a white Ford pickup that even at this distance looked muddy and well used, and a dark BMW that equally, at this distance, looked gleaming and clean.

Aside from the one over the door, no lights were visible from the house. The glass in the windows was dark, as was the glass pane above the door. Dehan sniffed and said, "They're home."

I grinned at her. "You can smell them, Washoe?"

"No, Stone, I can smell the smoke coming from the chimney." She pointed up at the tall black silhouette just visible against the icy stars. She placed her hands on the gate and in a single, fluid movement vaulted over it. I clambered over slightly less gracefully, and we headed across the blacktop toward the door. I hammered with my knuckles, and Dehan rang the bell.

Nothing happened, so we did it again. Third time around, a dull glow appeared in the glass above the door, and within we heard movement and footsteps approaching. Then the latch clunked and the door opened inward a few inches, secured by a chain. Sebastian Copes' long, boney face peered out at us.

"What the hell are you doing here?"

There was a whiff of alcohol on his breath. I gave him what I hoped was an amiable smile. "Is Angela Inglewood with you, Mr. Copes?"

"You want to explain how that's any of your business? I told you once before, if you want to communicate with me, you do it through my attorney!"

He was about to close the door, but Dehan cut him short. "Did you manage to find your son, Sebastian?"

He didn't answer, but he didn't close the door either. His eyes flicked over her, then he looked at me. "What's this about? First you ask about Angela, then my son . . ."

I gave a small shrug. "It's about Angela and your son. That's what it was always about, wasn't it?"

His eyes seemed to rove my face, then he turned back to Dehan. "My son is fine. He's been sick, but he's in good hands and he's recovering."

Before Dehan could answer I said, "That's good news. Can we come in?"

"No."

"We really need to talk to you. More to the point, Mr. Copes, you need to talk to us."

"I'm done with your threats."

"Where is your son, Sebastian?" It was Dehan. "You say he's fine, but where is he?"

"Do you have a warrant?"

"What for? We just want to know he's all right."

His voice was beginning to rise. "I'm his father, for God's sake! I'm telling you he's fine!"

I shook my head. "Fine, but where is Angela?"

"How should I know!"

"She's here, with you, isn't she, Mr. Copes?"

He swallowed hard. "Why would you say that?"

I gave a small laugh. "Because her car is parked just down the road."

He froze. "What?"

"Her car, Mr. Copes. Her car is parked just over there." I gestured in the general direction of Pussys Pond. "A cream Volkswagen GTI, you want the registration? We know she's here, Mr. Copes."

I paused. He stared hard at me. I sighed.

"Let me put it another way. This is a homicide investigation. You are a person of interest. We believe Angela Inglewood is in your house, and you are refusing to give us access to her. That's enough, Mr. Copes."

"What are you talking about?"

"It's enough to get a court order to search your home. We can camp out here until the paperwork is done and then you'll have all of East Hampton Police Department, and probably Suffolk County too, crawling all over your house."

"I don't believe you."

Dehan snorted. "You don't need to, Sebastian. You just need

to be not quite sure. Make life easy for yourself. Let us in. We just want to talk. If we wanted anything more, this place would be like a Kevlar fashion display by now."

He hesitated, then slipped the chain and stepped back, pulling the door with him. We went in.

We were in a hallway with a set of double doors on the left, and beyond them a broad, wooden staircase rising to a galleried landing. Two more doors were set in the wall on the right, and a passage that led to the back of the house. He pointed to the double doors. "In there."

As he said it the doors opened, and Angela stood looking out at us. The light of the room behind her was brighter than the dull light of the hall, so she was partly in silhouette. Her voice was dull, like the light.

"What are you doing here?"

Dehan answered. "Looking for you."

"Why?"

"You've had a busy day, Angela. We'd like to know what you've been doing."

"It's none of your concern."

I crossed the hall toward her, and she backed away into the room, so that now the light fell across her face. I could see fear in her eyes. When she spoke, her voice was a hoarse whisper. "You should leave."

I stepped through the door into a comfortable, old-fashioned drawing room. There was a big fireplace, five foot, with a solid oak beam across the top. Big logs were burning in the grate. The heavy, hardwood planks on the floor were polished to a shine and strewn with rugs. The armchairs and the sofa were of old, soft leather, cracked and creased, but comfortable. I took in the room and frowned at her.

"What makes you say that, Mrs. Inglewood?"

I heard the door close behind me and turned to look. Dehan was leaning against it with her arms crossed. Sebastian was crossing the room toward the fireplace with his long, stooping gait. He folded himself into a chair and scowled resentfully at me.

"All right, you're in now. What do you want?" Before I could answer he shifted his scowl to Angela and snapped, "Sit down, will you!"

She clenched her hands in front of her belly, chewing her lip, still watching me. Then dropped her gaze to the floor and crossed to the sofa, to sit beside Copes.

I made my way to the other chair and sat, waved a finger, gesturing at both of them.

"I'm interested, really quite curious." I looked up at the ceiling, remembering. "Um, let me see if I can recall. There was, 'I, frankly, could not give a damn about that gold-digging bitch and her lies.' And then there was, 'I got over Angela a long time ago . . . And I will never forgive that bitch for her callous, coldhearted betrayal.'" I raised my eyebrows and looked from Angela to Sebastian. "Care to explain?"

It was Sebastian who answered. "I don't have to explain anything to you or to anybody."

"I wouldn't be too sure about that, Mr. Copes. I keep telling you this is a homicide investigation."

His face contracted with irritation and flushed red. "But what has that got to do with me? With us? If I had wanted to kill Chuck or whatever the hell his name was, I would have done it twenty years ago! Not now!"

I heard Dehan's boots behind me, and after a moment she sat on the arm of the sofa.

"That doesn't necessarily follow, Sebastian. All you're really saying is that you had a motive twenty years ago, which you didn't act on. But, from what we're seeing now . . ." She gestured at the two of them with her finger. "Maybe a new motive has developed in the meantime."

"That's ridiculous. Angela only . . ."

"Seb!" She cut him short, and they glanced at each other. She looked down at her hands in her lap, and he at the fire, before going on. "We have only very recently got in touch again."

"Really," I said. I turned to Angela. "So what made you get in touch with Sebastian, Angela?"

She didn't say anything, and after a moment he answered for her.

"I guess your turning up, stirring everything up again, brought back memories . . ." He hesitated, did a strange little dance with his head. "Though . . . though I never really forgot."

Dehan made a small guffaw. "Seems you forgot pretty quickly what a gold-digging whore she was."

He scowled at her, but before he could answer I said, "I'm going to ask you once again where your son is, Sebastian."

"I told you he's in good hands."

I nodded. "I know he is no longer at risk . . ."

His scowl deepened. "What do you mean, 'no longer at risk'? What is that supposed to mean?"

"What I am trying to get from you, Sebastian, is not *how* he is, but *where*? Is that difference clear to you? One more time, Sebastian: *Where* is your son?"

He closed his eyes and took a surprisingly deep breath for such a skinny chest.

"He is at Angela's house."

Angela gave a small gasp and stared at him. Dehan narrowed her eyes and said, "Does that surprise you, Angela?"

Angela stared at her a moment, then down at her lap. Sebastian ignored them both and went on.

"He has been unwell, for some time. Ever since he was small, he has been troubled. And since his mid-teens he . . ."

I asked, "He missed his mother?"

He nodded. "He missed *a* mother. At school all the kids . . . You wouldn't believe. There are enough single mothers going around, but very few single fathers. And he wanted to know. Why didn't *he* have a mother? All the other kids had moms, why not him? And that hurt . . ."

Dehan asked, "Him or you?"

"It hurt us both. I found my anesthetic in work. But he, he searched in other, darker places."

"Drugs?"

He stared sullenly at the carpet. "Alcohol, dope, then coke. He loved coke. He progressed to harder stuff, crack and heroin, and . . ." He leaned his elbows on his knees and covered his face. "Sex, he was obsessed with sex. I tried. I really tried. I sent him to rehab, paid for the best psychiatrists. But it was like there was this black hole at the core of him, and whatever you gave him, whatever he took, it wasn't enough. He needed more."

"Where is he?"

He dropped his hands and narrowed his eyes at me. The resentment was a palpable thing in the air between us.

"You don't care, do you, Stone? All you care about is getting your man. His pain, the agony that conditions his actions, is not important to you. The pain that drives him to act as he does is irrelevant to you. Only one thing matters. Put him in cuffs and get him behind bars."

"I'm just curious about why you're hedging. How many times am I going to have to ask you before you give me an answer?"

"He is with his aunt."

I leaned back in my chair and looked across at Angela. She had gone very still and was staring at Sebastian.

Dehan said, "With his aunt? How many aunts has he got?"

He closed his eyes and shook his head. "There is my sister in San Francisco, but I mean Cathy. Angela's sister. He is with her."

I said, "Where, Sebastian?"

"At Angela's house. She is taking care of him there."

FOURTEEN

I stared at Dehan a long time. She stared back at me. It was a habit we had fallen into when we first started working together. It embarrassed the people around us, but it helped us think.

I spoke looking at Dehan, but then turned to frown at Sebastian Copes.

"So why is he at Angela's and not at Cathy's?"

"Well, obviously." He gave a small, impatient grunt. "He is Angela's son, he must be at Angela's house. Besides, I don't think Cathy's husband would appreciate having a sick lodger."

"And why not at your place? Surely..."

"Because I live in a luxurious bachelor pad on the Upper West Side. What is the *point* of these questions?"

"Who arranged all this? Just bear with me, Sebastian..."

"Stop *calling* me Sebastian!" He glared at Dehan. "And you too! We are *not* friends and we do *not* enjoy that familiarity! I am telling you that John is all right and being cared for! What *business* is it of yours who arranged it?"

I spoke quietly. "You can answer the question here, Mr. Copes, or you can answer it at the station. Who arranged this with Cathy?"

It was Angela who answered. Her cheeks, usually so white, were flushed, and her eyes were bright with tears.

"I did." She closed her eyes, gave a small sigh, and shook her head, like she was struggling to organize her thoughts. "It was between all of us, really. I . . ."

She took a deep breath and sagged back on the sofa.

"I was very stupid. We used to have a friend, many years ago, in Portland. She helped me, when Jonathan was born. She helped to find a clinic, and, may God forgive me, an orphanage. And surely everything that has happened has been God's punishment for my sins back then."

"What about your friend, Mrs. Inglewood?"

"She works at the orphanage where I left Jonathan. I did a very wicked thing, I went there to ask her . . ." She hesitated. "To ask her what had happened to my baby."

Dehan held up her right hand, pushing it slowly back and forth like she was pumping the brake on her car. "Slow down there a moment, Angela. Let's take this one step at a time. First of all, what made you do that?"

She pulled a handkerchief from her sleeve, blew her nose, and dabbed her eyes.

"You have to understand that we all, all of us, had this firmly behind us. And then you came along and started digging things up. When you spoke to Cathy, she told Patrick about your visit and he . . . He's an awful old busybody, and he told her that she should inform you about . . ." She raised her eyes and looked at Sebastian. "About what I had done twenty years ago. It brought everything back, and I started wondering, after all these years, what had happened to my son."

"Was that the only reason? Didn't you know already? Hadn't somebody told you, and you really went there to confirm what you had chosen till then not to believe?"

Sebastian erupted, "*Are you asking her or telling her? You're putting words into her mouth!*"

There was a sudden, leaden silence. Copes was scowling at

Dehan. Angela was motionless, with her hands on her lap and her eyes closed. The trail of a tear ran from the corner of her eye to the corner of her mouth.

"Before he died, Chuck told me that he knew Seb had used a private investigator to find out where I had left Jonathan, and he had gone there to get custody of him."

Dehan nodded once. "How did he come by this information?"

"He wouldn't say. I didn't believe it. I didn't want to believe it. But then when you barged in, opening up old wounds, stirring everything up again, the anxiety became too much and I drove up there and asked Mary to tell me if it was true. At first she refused, but I'm afraid I became hysterical. She ended up telling me."

I asked quietly, "What happened then?"

She realized too late that she had walked into a trap of her own making. She closed her eyes and covered her face. I prompted her. "Did you drive back to the Bronx?"

"No..."

Dehan said, "So you called? You called Cathy?"

"And you asked her to go and collect him?" Angela still had her eyes closed. She nodded. "There's just one thing I'm confused about, Angela." Angela didn't move. "How did you know where he was? Because Sebastian here had no idea. And we told you Gore was in the hospital, but you didn't know that Gore was your son, did you? For all those years, when he was going around to your sister's house, when Chuck beat seven bales of crap out of him, you didn't know that that was your son."

She shook her head but still kept her eyes closed.

"It was Chuck who told you, wasn't it?"

"Yes."

"How did he know?"

"He wouldn't tell me."

"He wouldn't tell you?" She shook her head. Dehan pressed her. "You see, here's what I am struggling with. What would make him tell you that Sebastian had collected your son from the orphanage and taken him home? What would make him tell you that that boy was Gore, and yet *not* tell you how he found out? I can't see the logic in that, can you?"

Now she opened her eyes, and there was a depth of pain in them. "Logic? You're looking for logic?" It was a strange echo of what she had said to me right at the beginning of the investigation. "Where is the logic in any of this? In a nineteen-year-old child being raped and infected with HIV? In a good, honorable man being stabbed to death in his home in the middle of the afternoon? There is no sense or logic; these are the trials the Lord sends us, and all we can do is suffer them."

I smiled and tried to make it look sympathetic. "Those are moving words, Mrs. Inglewood, and believe me, I do sympathize. But still, I take my partner's point. It is hard to visualize that situation. Perhaps you can help us. How did it happen? How did it come about?"

She spread her hands and her arms, like she was embracing helplessness, then let them drop in her lap.

"It was . . ." Her eyes became abstracted. "It was very shortly before he died. We were preparing for bed. We were talking about something quite different, I can't recall what, and he suddenly said, 'Angie, there is something I need to tell you. It's the reason I got so angry with Gore, and beat him so severely. He is the boy you gave up for adoption. Your boss, Sebastian Copes, collected him from the orphanage after you left him.' And then he gripped my hand and said, "But you have to understand, Angie, he knows. He knows you're his mother.'" She opened her hands, as though she might find his hand still held there, and said simply, "And that was it."

"You didn't question him further?"

"Of course I did."

"You asked how he knew?"

"Yes."

"And what did he say?"

Her breath started to shake; her eyes became red and spilled tears. Her voice came twisted with emotion. "He said Gore had told him! That Gore had been blackmailing him. If he didn't give him money, he would tell me and Sadie who he was. And Chuck had wanted to protect me from the pain . . ."

Dehan leaned forward, her face screwed up, shaking her head. "Why didn't you tell us all this? Can you not see how *important* this is?"

"*Yes!*" She turned her back and walked away. "*Yes, of course I can!*" Then more quietly, into her hands, "It's because of that that I wanted to hide from it, and hope it would all just go away! I never meant for *any* of this to happen!"

I looked at Dehan. She had an "I told you so" eyebrow raised at me.

"So let me get this straight," I said. "How long before he was killed did Chuck land this information on you?"

"I can't remember exactly. But it was almost immediately before."

I turned to Sebastian. "Did you know about this?"

"No. I had no idea. He had told me once or twice that he would like to meet his biological mother. That was when he was younger. When he got older he stopped talking about it, but I guess he was still curious. He . . ." He glanced at Angela and then looked down at his hands. "He was pretty bitter about it." He shrugged. "It would have been easy for him to find out who she was, either from company records, employees, or even from the orphanage. But he never told me. The truth is that from the age of sixteen onward he never told me anything."

I scratched my head, frowning hard. "So, when exactly did you find out that your son had made contact with his mother and was hanging out with Sadie?"

"Today."

"How?"

"Angela contacted me at the office. I couldn't believe it at first, but then I thought it was probably something to do with the investigation and all the *shit* that you were stirring up. So I had my secretary put her through. Then she told me. She told me everything."

"Everything?"

"About how Jonathan had sought them out . . ."

Dehan said, "What do you mean by that?"

"He had started frequenting the same bars and hangouts as Sadie and her friends, practically forcing himself on the group."

Dehan glanced at Angela. Angela nodded. "It meant nothing to me at the time, but I remember her telling me this new boy had started hanging around with them. Adriel didn't like him. I guess he was jealous. Sadie didn't like him to begin with, but bit by bit he had started to grow on her." She had been standing with her back to us, staring out the black glass of the window. Now she closed the drapes and returned to the sofa. As she sat she said, "He had a kind of charm. We all found him annoying, but he ingratiated himself with all of us . . ."

"Except Chuck."

"Yes, except Chuck. Even before he knew who he was, Gore got Chuck's hackles up. It was like an instinct."

I looked at Copes for a moment. "There's something on my mind, Mr. Copes."

"Isn't there always."

"Two, two and a half years ago, Jonathan came home one day with a broken jaw, four fractured ribs . . ."

"He didn't come home. The hospital contacted me and told me my son had had a bad accident. I went immediately and saw that he was in a terrible state. His face was a mess, and his entire body was black and blue. He told the doctor that he had fallen down some stairs. But she, the doctor, took me aside and told me that she did not believe it. She could not compel him to tell the truth, obviously—I mean, what are they going to do? Torture him? I mean, that would defeat the very *point* . . ."

"Mr. Copes?"

He rubbed his face with his large, boney hands. He sighed, and the air trembled in his throat.

"Anyway! They could not *compel* him to tell the truth, but the doctor was pretty certain that he had been beaten up. I took him home and arranged for the best medical treatment, and asked him *what* had *happened*. I told him, 'What do you want? You want a bike? You want a Les Paul? You, you . . .'" He got stuck on the "you" and repeated it three times in rapid succession. "'You-you-you want a holiday in the Caribbean? *What do you want?*'" He held up two fists, as though he was clutching at his son's lapels. "'*Just tell me who did this?*' But he wouldn't."

"You knew he was hanging out with new friends."

He shook his head, shrugged, spread his arms wide.

"Yes. Yes, he mentioned some names of kids he was hanging with. But honestly? You know, I had so much work, we connected so little, I barely even registered the fact."

I decided to play a hunch. "How long," I said, and leaned back, staring at the wall behind Copes' head. "How long do you think it would take us to find out if you employed a private detective around the time Jonathan started hanging out with Sadie Byrne?"

There was a deathly silence in the room. Angela looked genuinely astonished. So did Dehan. Copes stared at me for a long time, then shifted his gaze to the fire.

"I don't know. I should have thought that would be quite difficult. In any case, what makes you think . . ."

"Well, I know you used one to find out where Angela was giving birth, and where she was going to leave the baby. So if you were worried about your son, and I have no doubt you were very worried about your son, wouldn't it be logical to use one again? In fact"—I gave a small laugh—"two gets you twenty you use private detectives quite a bit. Something tells me you are that kind of guy. Let me tell you, Mr. Copes. It would be as easy as subpoenaing your bank records for the period when Jonathan started hanging out with Sadie. Hey, you were looking out for your son."

I waited. He said nothing until Dehan asked, "How long was it before you realized he was hanging out with Angela's niece?"

He leaned forward with his hands over his head. The gesture made him look oddly like a chimpanzee.

"I wanted to know if he was taking drugs. I wanted to know if he was doing anything dangerous, that he could get hurt or wind up in jail. A man has to look out for his son. I mean, show me! Show me *anywhere* where it says it's wrong for a man to protect his *fucking children*!"

"Take it easy, Mr. Copes. Just tell me what happened. He came back to you with the report . . ."

"He already knew. It's the guy I always use. I'd been using him for years. He was the guy who followed Angela to Portland. He came and he told me, 'Your son has gone and found his birth mother.' Birth mother. I mean, what kind of mother is he going to have? That's what your mother is, right? It's the woman who gives *birth to you*!"

He stood up and strode around the room, not quite going anywhere. He came to a halt in front of the fireplace. I said, "So you had a decision to make."

"I decided to ignore it and get on with my work."

Dehan made a loud "Ha!" sound, and he turned to stare at her. His lip curled and his nostrils flared.

"What the hell do you mean, 'Ha!'"

"Why don't you tell us what else your private dick unearthed while he was spying on Jonathan?"

"I don't know what you're talking about."

She turned to Angela. "How about you, Angela? Are you going to tell us what else was going on between Haviland Avenue and Powell Avenue?"

She gave her head a small shake. "I don't know what you're referring to."

Dehan sighed. "How long did you have Jonathan under surveillance?"

"That time, about a month."

"And in that time, your detective didn't notice anything peculiar going on?"

"Yes, he did. God, you people!" He stared at me resentfully. "Do you have to drag this up? Hasn't she been through enough?"

I said, "Say it."

He turned and looked at Angela. "I'm sorry. I didn't want you to know, but these *people* . . . Chuck was having an affair."

Her face seemed to crumple. Tears spilled from her eyes and traced ragged lines down her cheeks.

"Who . . . ?"

"Your sister, Cathy."

FIFTEEN

Sebastian Copes rose to his feet. For a moment he seemed to be too big for the room as he rushed to the sofa, all arms, legs, and angles. He sat next to Angela and didn't so much embrace her as engulf her in his arms. She didn't hug him back but allowed herself to be held. Dehan rose and went to stand beside the fire.

Angela buried her face in Sebastian's chest, and he turned a twisted, bitter face toward me. "What do you *want* from us? Go *away*! Leave us *alone*! All we ever wanted was to be *alone*! *Together!*"

And then he was sobbing convulsively and noisily. His face swelled, as though he had a bad cold. I watched Angela's arms slide around him, hesitate, and then cling hard.

I looked up at Dehan. She puffed out her cheeks and blew softly.

They stayed like that for five long minutes. Eventually Sebastian turned to look at me, but he didn't let go of Angela.

"Will you please leave. I don't know what you came here to do, but you have caused nothing but pain and hurt. We are trying to heal, to recover." His face flushed red in one of his surges of rage. "I *think* even *we* are entitled to heal, aren't we?"

I nodded. "Sure."

"Then please, take your partner, and your *malicious, destructive* intentions, and *leave*!"

I paused a moment, looking at the floor, wondering exactly how to proceed. I said, "We will. We'll go. But before we do, we have some information which is very important for both of you."

He let go of her. She sat back on the sofa, pulling her handkerchief from her sleeve. He turned to face me. "Is this another one of your subtle ploys, Detective Stone?"

"No." I shifted my gaze to Angela. She was staring at her handkerchief as she folded and unfolded it, searching for a dry spot. "All my endeavors so far, Mr. Copes, Mrs. Inglewood, have been to find the person who raped Sadie and murdered your husband. That is not a malicious or destructive thing to do, is it?"

He stared at me for a long moment, and when it came, his voice was a rasp. "Tell us what you need to tell us, and then leave."

I pointed at Angela. "You came here directly, Mrs. Inglewood? Directly from Portland?"

She nodded and gave a small, wet "Yes."

"But you had spoken to Mr. Copes earlier, before you went."

"Yes."

"So, at what time, precisely, did Cathy go and collect Jonathan?"

"I don't know . . ."

I turned to Sebastian. "At what time did you know that they were going to go to Angela's house?"

He scowled, confused. "Just after midday, why? You said you were going to *tell* us something! This is not *telling*! This is *asking*! I mean, you must know the difference! For Christ's sake! Telling is when you *impart* . . ."

"Mr. Copes. Be quiet." I held his eye a moment. "If you will be quiet for just one moment, I will tell you what it is I came here to tell you. I just need to be clear about something. The chronology here is that you, Mrs. Inglewood, called Mr. Copes late morning and told him that you were going to Portland. You drove up there, spoke to Mary Finch, and confirmed what Chuck had told you, then you telephoned Cathy and told her to collect Jonathan, and you called Mr. Copes and told him what you had discovered and what you had done. Is that correct?"

She glanced at Sebastian and nodded. He nodded too. "Yes."

"Then you, Mrs. Inglewood, came directly here from Portland, and you, Mr. Copes, finished work and came from there, via Throggs Neck."

"Yes."

I glanced at Dehan. She was frowning hard and shaking her head. I said:

"I have to tell you, Mrs. Inglewood, Mr. Copes, that Jonathan was found murdered this afternoon, in your house, Mrs. Inglewood."

Angela covered her mouth with both hands. Her eyes were wide and stared at Sebastian. His long arms and legs began to tremble. He tried to stand, but his legs gave out from under him. His face was a mauve color, and his lips were quivering as he tried to speak. All he could say was, "No, no, no . . ."

I kept going, watching them both. "He was not alone. He was with Cathy."

He exploded, "*That bitch killed him! She killed my son! Why? Why did she kill him?*"

Angela was clawing at his arm. "No, no, Sebastian. No, no, it can't be! It's a mistake!"

I said, "I don't know if she killed your son, but if she did, somebody else killed her."

Angela froze. Sebastian went still, but his lips and his hands were still trembling. "What . . . ? What are you talking about . . . ?"

"Do you still stick to your story, Mr. Copes, that you received those three telephone calls from Mrs. Inglewood, and then you drove out to Long Island, via Throgs Neck Bridge, passing just three or four hundred yards from Mrs. Inglewood's house, where

Cathy and Jonathan were found dead, killed with the same weapon? Is that the story you want to stick to?"

He stared at me for a long time. Then he blinked and stared at the fire instead. Angela had pulled away from him, up against the arm of the sofa. Her eyes were wide with terror. Her voice had an edge of hysteria to it. "Sebastian?" She stood and backed away toward the wall. "*Sebastian?*" He said nothing, and then she screamed. It was a ghastly, shattering noise like nails on glass. "*Sebastian! Sebastian! Sebastian! Sebastian!*" over and over until Dehan jumped to her feet and Angela collapsed to her knees.

Sebastian was grunting, covering his ears with his long hands, struggling to get to his feet. His eyes were wild, unseeing. I stood too. He lunged toward me, not because he was trying to hit me, but because he had no control over his legs, which were shaking badly. He gripped my shoulder.

"It's too much," he said. "Do you understand that?"

"Yes."

"It's too much. A person can't take that much. You . . ." He kind of laughed, but without amusement, and waggled his fingers at the side of his head. "You begin to crack under the strain. I think . . ." He gripped both my shoulders with his hands. "Listen to me. I think that's what happened, to Jonathan. I think he . . ." Again he waggled his fingers, his face twisted in a frown, like he was searching for a word. "He . . . he *cracked*, you know, like his head split open. Because you *can't keep losing love!*" He laughed, like he thought he'd hit the nail on the head. He liked the phrase. "*You can't keep losing love!*"

His shoulders began to shake. His bottom lip curled in, and then his whole body trembled. Then his face clenched like a fist on a nail and he was bellowing at the top of his lungs, "*You can't keep losing love! You can't keep losing love! For God's sake! You can't keep on losing love . . .*"

I tried to take a hold of him and sit him down, but he was huge and gangly and out of control. I was trying to push him toward a chair, and he was trying to grip me, push me, pull me, and get me to look at him all at the same time, all while wailing and screaming. I wound up stumbling, losing my balance, and falling. I cracked my head on the stone hearth and for a moment I was dazed and foggy. It felt like somebody had driven an iron chisel through my skull. I lifted my head and saw Sebastian striding toward the door shouting, "*Jonathan! Jonathan! My son! I am sorry! I love you . . . !*"

Then Dehan was bounding after him like a gazelle, muttering, "Son of a bitch!"

I struggled to my feet and felt a warm trickle of blood slip down the back of my neck. The floor made like a boat on the high seas, and my stomach rose to meet the throbbing in my head. I fought down the nausea and leaned on the back of one of the large leather chairs.

Angela was sitting huddled on the floor in the corner, watching me with frightened eyes.

"He killed them," she said simply, and the words sounded damp. Her face was damp; her eyes and nose were pink. I realized I was concussed, but a voice in my head told me I had to get it together because this was no time for a concussion. I held out my hand.

"Come on, we'd better go."

"He'll kill you too."

"No, he won't. Statistically it's impossible. Give me your hand."

"What?"

I sighed. My head really hurt, and I really wanted her to give me her hand. But I said, "I can trace my ancestors back to microbial life forms that inhabited this planet four point five billion years ago. And look, we're still here. So statistically, the chances of Sebastian finishing that line off are incalculably small. Now give me your hand, Angela. Let's get you somewhere safe."

She gave that frown women give when they have absolutely

no idea what you're talking about, and reached out her hand. I took it and pulled her gently to her feet. She clung to me suddenly, and violent pain surged through my head, causing another wave of nausea. I fought it down again but felt how the blood drained from my face and my head.

We moved toward the door. I strained my hearing for any sign of Dehan or Sebastian, but I could hear nothing. We squeezed through the double doors, which still stood open, and crossed the hall toward the front door. It also stood open, and the cool night air wafted in.

We stepped out. I felt suddenly cold and shuddered, and leaned against the doorjamb. Somewhere an owl cried out, and I tried to remember what the difference was between the male and the female cry. Angela was holding my waist, looking up into my face. She looked more scared now than before.

"I'll be okay," I said. "We need to find Dehan."

She shook her head. "No, we need to find Sebastian. He is dangerous." Her face was at risk of crumpling again. "He killed my Chuck, in that cruel, cruel way. And he killed my baby. If only I had known . . ."

She leaned against me and started to sob. I gave her a squeeze and said, "Okay, Angela. Hold it together till we get back to town. We have to pull together and be strong. Let's get to the car."

We staggered across the yard. I leaned on her as much as I tried to support her. A couple of times the ground seemed to rise up and then fall away beneath me. Then we stopped, and she steadied me. And after a moment we moved on.

Finally we came to the gate. I smiled. "I'm not going to vault it."

She ignored me, unlatched it, and swung it open. The great, dark, yawning space it left destabilized me and I staggered. Angela was there, then, with her arm around my waist, guiding me toward the Jag on the far side of the road.

A shout, indistinct, maybe beyond the trees. Female. Not

Sebastian's baritone. Angela was clinging to my jacket, staring fearfully past my shoulder.

"Do you have a gun?"

I fumbled in my pocket for the key, slipped it in the lock. "Get in the back."

"No! Don't leave me alone. He'll come back for me." She clawed at my chest. "He killed Chuck, then he killed Gore, now he'll come for me."

"Get in the back, lie down. I'll lock the car. He won't be able to get in."

"He'll smash the windows!"

"They're bulletproof," I lied. "I have to go get him. I have to help Dehan." She hesitated. I snarled, "Get in!"

"You have a gun?"

"Of course! Now get in, Angela! And stay out of sight. Don't look out the windows."

She crawled in and lay down on the back seat. Unless somebody came right up and peered in, in the darkness, she was invisible. I locked the door and headed for the dark mass of trees that separated the house and the road from the shores of Napeague Bay.

I stepped into the darkness, in among the close shadows of the trees, and heard my footfalls, loud, rustling, and snapping as I trod on leaves and twigs. Branches touched my face, others pulled at my jacket and my shirt as I eased my way along. I have no idea if I went ten yards or a hundred. The darkness was so dense, the trees so close and indistinguishable one from another. Ferns brushed at my legs, sometimes waist deep. Large branches blocked my path, forcing me to duck under them or clamber over them. I might have walked in circles for hours among the rustles and crackles, and the eerie cries of the night birds.

Only one thing guided me: the distant whisper of the water. That and the cool breeze that touched my face, which I knew came from the ocean. That was the direction from which I had heard the cry. So that was where I had to go.

My head still throbbed, and my stomach was still nauseous, but I fought to ignore both and focused my mind on Dehan.

Eventually the trees thinned out and I found myself in an area of open ground surrounded by the inky silhouettes of the trees against the starlit sky. I could make out an indistinct path —more like the space between areas of woodland, overgrown with weeds and ferns. I called out Dehan's name and set off at a stumbling run toward what looked like a gap in the dark shapes of the trees. From there I could hear the soft lap and sigh of the water on the shore. I called again as I ran, but there was no reply.

Panic started to uncoil in my belly. If she was not here, then where? If they were both gone, then where had they gone? Where should I look for her?

I broke out of the trees and found I was on the shore, a sloping strip of land, maybe fifty or sixty yards from the water's edge.

"*Dehan!*"

Only the sigh of the water answered. I ran across the uneven, rutted ground. Fell to my knees and struggled to rise. Ran again and called out into the darkness: "*Dehan! Dehan!*"

Behind and beyond the soft splash of the small waves, the whisper of the breeze among the pines, and the lonesome cry of the owl, there was an absolute, crushing silence. A silence that was large, heavy, and black. I took two more steps, bellowing her name, then fumbled in my pocket for my cell.

Calling her on the phone was a bad idea, because if Copes had turned dangerous and she was hidden from him, the ring would give her position away. But what was even more dangerous was not knowing where she was or what had happened to her. I pressed her number and almost immediately I heard it ring. It was up ahead of me, beyond a low rise in the shore. I ran.

I ran stumbling, and beyond the rise, the ocean appeared, vast and luminous with starlight, the orange ooze of the moon swelling over the horizon. The ringing was coming from beside the shore. I ran, stumbled, fell, clawed my way to my feet again, and stopped dead, three paces from the lapping waves.

Her cell was lying in the mud, pulsing light as it rang. I bent and picked it up. I hung up and the ringing stopped, leaving a backwash of silence that engulfed me. I scoured the dark, amorphous forms around me but found no sign of Dehan. I called her name but got no reply.

Then I saw the body, in the growing light of the moon. It wasn't lying on the shore; it was standing, fifty or sixty feet away, knee-deep in the semi-fluorescent wash of the ocean. It was the tall, angular form of Sebastian Copes. I called out his name, but he seemed not to hear. I ran, stumbling, calling to him, but he just stood, motionless, looking out at the rising moon.

I waded out into the cold water, stood beside him, and gripped his arm.

"Sebastian! For God's sake! What are you doing?"

He turned his face to me, like I'd appeared out of nowhere. It was twisted, tortured with nameless pain. His mouth hung open and he was moaning incoherent sounds, keening like an oversize baby.

"Sebastian! *Sebastian!* Look at me! *Look at me!* Do you know who I am?"

The icy water lapped around us. He took one slow step and turned toward me. His face was sodden with tears and grief. He placed his large hands on my shoulders and a long, agonizing, keening noise emitted from his throat as he began to bend double. Among the excruciating noise were words.

"I killed him . . ." He gazed into my eyes, begging me to tell him it wasn't true, it was going to be okay. But I knew nothing was ever going to be okay again for this poor bastard.

"I killed him . . ." he said again.

"Come on, Sebastian, let's go back to the shore."

"No, no." He shook his head. "I have to die. I can't . . . it's too much. I have to die too . . ."

I grabbed his arms and tried to pull him toward the shore. He resisted, and for a moment we struggled. I lost my footing and slipped under the water. For a second everything was liquid silence. I felt his hands tighten on my lapels. He pulled, I found my footing, and as I emerged from the water he seemed to jerk.

I shouted at him, *"For God's sake, Sebastian! We have to go back!"*

And that was when I saw the dark stain on his shirt, on his chest, and he began to sink.

SIXTEEN

I dragged savagely at him, screaming at him, "*Walk! Walk! Goddamn it! Walk!*"

I heard the crashing and splashing of feet charging into the water, and Dehan's voice bellowing, "*Stone! Stone! Are you okay? Stone, for crying out loud!*"

"Help me drag him to the shore! Did you shoot him?"

"He was drowning you!"

We heaved him with huge difficulty through the muddy water until we could lay him on the shore. I wiped water from my eyes and felt the pulse in his neck. It was faint. Dehan felt her pockets. "I dropped my phone..."

I pulled it from my sodden pocket and handed it to her. "Why didn't you answer me? I was shouting your name..."

"I did. You couldn't hear me." She was dialing. "Where's Angela?" Before I could answer she snapped into the phone, "This is Detective Carmen Dehan, NYPD. I urgently need two ambulances at..."

She gave them the address and explained where we were. When she'd hung up she scowled at me.

"You okay?"

I nodded. I was beginning to shiver with cold. "Yeah, I got a bit concussed. There was a bit of blood, but I seem to be okay now. I put Angela in the back of the Jag. We ought to get to her. I was worried about you. You wouldn't answer me."

"You are soaking. You're also concussed."

"I said that."

She smiled. "You're talking like you were drunk."

I lowered myself onto the dry mud and hugged my knees. "As if," I said. "As if you were drunk. What happened to you?"

She pulled off her jacket and draped it over Sebastian.

"I thought he was going to try to escape. So I went after him, but I expected him to go for the car. Instead he dodged through the trees toward the beach. He must know this place like the back of his hand. I lost him straightaway. In the end I was running around like a headless chicken, wondering what the hell had happened to you and why you weren't with me. I kept falling over on this damned ground. It's so full of damned holes it's like the surface of the moon!"

"You lost your phone," I said, with chattering teeth.

"I know that. You gave it to me."

"I know. I gave it to you."

"So next thing I see you and Sebastian struggling in the water. I ran to help you, and next thing he has you under the water and he's holding you down. So I plugged him. I tried to plug him in the shoulder, but he was moving, it was dark, and I was running."

"Yeah." I nodded. "We'll see what the doctors say. Let's hope he pulls through."

They didn't take long. A couple of minutes later a procession of lights and sirens approached from the south. We watched them reflected in the water, disappearing behind the trees and the houses, and a couple of minutes later the flashlights appeared, bouncing and dancing through the undergrowth. We called to them and put our phones on flashlight to guide them toward us.

There were four uniformed officers. One of them was a sergeant with a sour face, and behind them there were a bunch of paramedics with two gurneys. I waved my arms.

"No," I said, aware that I was being slightly incoherent, "the second one, the second gurney, is for the woman in the burgundy Jaguar back at the house..."

The sergeant and a couple of the paramedics stopped and looked at me. My clothes were soaking and sagging around my legs, and I was shivering with the cold. The sergeant turned to Dehan. "Is this man all right?"

I snarled at him, "I am Detective John Stone! Of course I am all right!" I pointed at Sebastian's motionless form on the shore. "*That* man is in urgent need of medical assistance. He's been shot! There is another woman in the back of the Jaguar you must have parked next to, and she is in shock. You need to go and help her."

The rear gurney and three of the paramedics started back.

"Wait!" I called, wishing I could remember how to speak normally. "You'll need the keys."

They rattled as I handed them over, and the small group departed at an awkward trot, glancing at each other. I returned to where the remaining paramedics were hunkered around Sebastian.

"How is he?"

"Hard to tell." It was a girl with a blond ponytail, who looked too young to be doing what she was doing. "The shot was through and through..." She glanced at Dehan. "You shot him?"

"Yeah, nine-millimeter."

The paramedic gave her head a little sideways twist. "Impossible to say how much damage it's done, and in this light how much blood he's lost. Let's get him to the hospital and into surgery."

They lifted him onto the gurney and started trundling him awkwardly across the rutted earth toward the house. The sergeant stood in front of me.

"You need medical attention?"

"No." I shook my head and wiped water from my forehead. "It's just a bit of concussion."

"Good. So I can tell you this. When I said you could come

and talk to these people. That didn't mean it was okay for you to come and terrorize them and start shooting them."

Before I could answer, Dehan barked at him, "Hey! Sergeant! My partner is concussed because that man they just took away on the gurney knocked his head against a hearthstone and then tried to drown him. Here he may be all kinds of old money, blue blood, and good people. But in the Bronx, so far, he has killed three people, and his fourth was about to be a cop. We came here to talk, and talk is what we did. And while we were talking we were assaulted, and an attempt was made on Detective Stone's life. So how about you pipe down, quit griping, and offer some support to your fellow officers?" She turned to me. "Come on, Stone. Let's get the hell out of here."

We moved away. Behind us I could hear Sergeant Whatever-hisnamewas shouting, "Hey! You can't just walk away!"

Dehan snarled over her shoulder, "You'll receive our statements and our reports tomorrow, if not later!"

By the time we got back to the house Angela was sitting in the back of one of the ambulances, wrapped in a blanket. She was talking to a paramedic, shaking her head.

"No, I don't want a tranquilizer. I just want to go home."

Dehan glanced up at me. "You should have them look at you, and get some dry clothes."

I shook my head, like Angela. "No. When we get back. When everything is settled."

The sergeant and his men appeared through the trees. I stepped over to him. "Sergeant..."

"Grimes."

"Sergeant Grimes, that man..." I pointed at Copes as he was being lifted into the back of the ambulance. "He needs to be under twenty-four-hour-a-day police guard until we can get him back to the Bronx."

There was something of a sneer about his smile. "You still a bit concussed, Detective? He ain't going nowhere."

I gave him the dead eye, no expression whatsoever. "Did I ask for your opinion, Sergeant?"

He didn't answer, so I kept waiting. Eventually he looked down at his shoes and said, "We don't have that kind of resources."

"I want a twenty-four-hour police guard on that man, sitting beside his bed. I do not want him left alone. I will have my chief call your chief to arrange it, and I will make a point of mentioning how cooperative you were, Sergeant Grimes. In the meantime, that man is suicidal, and if I lose my prisoner, I will know whom to hold responsible. Now do your damned job and escort that man to the hospital."

He spat at my feet and made his way to his car.

The first ambulance, with Sebastian Copes in it, pulled away, escorted by the two patrol cars. We joined Angela then at the back of the second ambulance. The paramedic, a young guy with long red hair and wire glasses, shrugged at me as he closed up his kit.

"Not much I can do here, boss. She's not hurt. More scared than anything. She won't take a tranquilizer, and she won't come in to the hospital. She just wants to go home. And Andy says that's probably the best thing for her."

"Who's Andy?"

"Me. If there's nothing wrong with her, we can't take her to the Bronx. Can you give her a ride?"

"Sure. No problem."

He slammed the doors, they clambered aboard, and they took off into the night.

We stood a moment in awkward silence, watching the red taillights disappear up the lane. Then Angela sighed, with a bit of a shudder in it, and glanced at the house, with the door still standing open.

"I suppose we had better close up before we leave." Then she glanced at Dehan like she needed permission. "I wouldn't mind a cup of coffee before we go. It's getting cold."

I nodded agreement. "And, as you're driving, I could use something a little stronger."

"Okay, and I'm going to find you some dry clothes. You'll catch pneumonia if you don't change soon."

We pushed open the gate and made our way across the yard, then into the house. We didn't return to the living room. Angela led the way down the short corridor to the right of the hall and into a large, old-fashioned country kitchen. Dehan pointed to a chair at the large old wooden table and said, "Sit! I'm going to get you some towels and some clothes from upstairs."

I groaned and sat with my hands covering my eyes. I heard Angela say, "What does he drink, whiskey? In the living room, in the cabinet."

I heard Dehan leave, uncovered my eyes, and watched Angela awhile making the coffee.

"You seem to know this house pretty well."

She smiled without looking at me. "I suppose I do. It's a long time ago, twenty years, but it feels like yesterday. We came here a few times."

My phone rang. I pulled it from my wet pocket, wiped the screen, and answered.

"John? It's Joe."

"Hey."

"Can you talk?"

"Sure. Shoot. What is it?"

"I got the results from the sheets."

"Uh-huh . . ."

"It was positive. Did you know?"

"I guessed. It was the only way it made sense."

"Really? I don't see it."

"I'll explain it when you invite us for dinner. I heard your wife makes the best lasagna in the Western Hemisphere."

He laughed. "Okay, I'll get her to call Dehan."

I thanked him and hung up. I heard feet tramping down the stairs, and a moment later Dehan came in with an armful of towels and clothes, which she dumped on the table. She also had a bottle of Glenfiddich single malt and a large tumbler.

She filled the glass and started toweling my hair so I couldn't drink. As she toweled she said, "The clothes are too big, but no one will see you till you get home."

By the time she had stripped me and redressed me in absurd clothes, I was on my second glass of single malt and feeling warmer and steadier. Angela sat and poured two large cups of coffee with milk for her and Dehan, and a small black one for me, which I laced liberally with Scotch. I drained the cup and sat up a second. When I was done I said, "The lab just called." Dehan looked at me curiously. I said, "The blood on the sheets, on the bed where Chuck was found, I had them check it. It came back positive for HIV."

There was a long, heavy silence. Dehan was frowning at the tabletop. Angela was staring unseeing at an invisible spot a couple of feet in front of her. Eventually Dehan shifted her gaze to me in a silent question. What did it mean?

I said, "It was the only way any of it made any sense. He was dying, and he knew it." I looked at Angela. "He raped Sadie, didn't he?" She nodded. I went on. "Everybody assumed that she got AIDS from her rapist. But it was the other way around. Her rapist got AIDS from her. And she wouldn't admit it was him who raped her, and he would not admit he'd got AIDS from her. I can only imagine they had a real close relationship all their lives, that went badly sour when she hit her late teens."

She drew a deep, shuddering breath. "He adored her from the day she was born. And she adored him. He was the best uncle in the world, because he desperately wanted a child, but we couldn't have one."

Dehan said, "But there are ways around that . . ."

"Not for him. It had to be his, the old-fashioned way, or not at all. That was the way he was. A bit raw, a bit primal, and that was his downfall. When Sadie turned sixteen she started to change. She became defiant, sarcastic, rude. She started to hang around with these *freaks* she called friends. We all tried to be tolerant and open-minded. Of course Patrick had no problem with that. As long as they leave him alone with his books he is the most tolerant, liberal man in the world. So while Sadie became more and more outrageous in her behavior, Patrick withdrew more and more into his den, and Cathy and I buried our heads deeper in the sand. Poor Chuck probably loved her better than any of us, and he wasn't even blood. He watched her decline, he railed at us, he used to give her the fiercest scoldings, and we just ignored him.

"And the more he scolded her, the more she provoked him. I think, at heart, that was what she wanted. She wanted somebody to care, and she thought we didn't. Because we did nothing to stop her. But he did. He was the only one who did."

She stared at the coffeepot and seemed to get lost. When I realized she'd stopped talking I said, "But things got confused. Adolescent kids, especially kids who use drugs, they lose the boundaries. She didn't understand why he was getting so mad at Gore. She thought he was jealous. She didn't realize that Gore was her first cousin. She had no idea, and of course Chuck did, because Gore had told him.

"Gore had sought you out, literally hunted you down, to punish you. He had inherited his father's crazy streak, and over the years, as he learned what had happened to him, he grew first to resent, and then to hate the woman who had abandoned him. He, like Sadie, got into hard drugs, and the more drugs he did, the closer he came to psychosis. We'll never know, but my guess was that he knew he had the virus and he deliberately gave it to Sadie.

"Meanwhile, Sadie was becoming more and more provocative with Chuck. I don't know if Chuck was a drinker..."

She shook her head. "No, but on the night in question he got drunk. Cathy and I were away visiting friends..."

"So he got himself drunk, probably agonizing over what was happening to her and in turmoil over the way she seemed to be coming on to him. It probably also drove him crazy to think of her sleeping with those weird creeps."

"It did. He used to rant and rave about it."

"So, once he was good and drunk, he did something really stupid. He went over to confront her. I'm guessing she was alone, and I figure this was just before he beat Gore up. He probably started by trying to reason with her, and two gets you twenty she laughed at him. She probably accused him of being jealous and he lost it and raped her. It is no excuse, rape is inexcusable, period. But he paid the price. Because shortly after that he discovered he had the virus. When did he tell you?"

"Not for months."

"He watched Sadie decline and die, and I imagine you all assumed the cooling of relations between them was because he had beaten up Gore. But it wasn't. It was because of the very dark secret that they both shared. He had raped her, and she had killed him."

We sat in silence for a while. The glass in the kitchen window looked very black, with very sad-looking ghosts held within it. I refilled my glass and took a deep breath.

"He confessed all of this to you."

"Yes."

"And at the same time he told you that Gore, Jonathan, had told him that he was yours and Sebastian's son. That Sebastian had collected him from the orphanage almost immediately after you had left him, that he had tracked you down, and that he had been blackmailing him for money for drugs."

"Yes."

I took another deep breath and said, "And he told you all this when he asked you to kill him."

I saw Dehan's eyes go wide as she turned to stare at me. But Angela simply gave a nod and said, "Yes."

"There is one thing I am not clear about, Angela. I know you loved Chuck very deeply. I know you were devoted to him. But when you killed him . . ." I hesitated. "I know you used a method which would be quick and comparatively painless. The scalpel, or whatever you used, was very sharp. He probably felt very little, but there was also a savage cruelty about it. Was it a mercy killing, or was it revenge?"

She took a long time to answer. When she did, her voice was very quiet. She said simply, "I don't know."

"It was a hell of a betrayal."

"I knew he had slept with Cathy. I didn't care about that—I felt I deserved it for what I had done with Sebastian. But Sadie . . ."

"You killed him in the morning."

"Yes."

"There was a lot of blood. You had to mop the floor and the bathroom to remove your footprints. You had to be very thorough indeed, and you were. Then you showered and washed the clothes. But you left traces of blood in the bathroom, behind the taps in the grout, and you forgot to take the clothes from the washing machine."

"I just wanted to get out of there."

"In the afternoon you took his phone with you to Mrs. Nowak's house. You went to the bathroom and you made several calls to your own telephone from his. When you returned, you pretended to hear it ringing, told her you had several calls from your husband and you had better get back. And that was when you called 911. How did you get his voice?"

"He was willing. Most of it was his plan. He recorded himself onto my phone, asking for help and saying the address. I made that call from the bathroom too, just before I left Violet's house. I knew I'd have to hurry, but I had a few minutes to get back and put his phone in his hand." She took a deep sigh. "It was horrible, watching him slip away. He would never have had time to make those calls. It was almost instant."

"Yeah, that troubled me. The blood loss must have been catastrophic." She looked at me with no particular expression and said nothing. "That much," I said, "I understood pretty quickly.

As I said, it was the only way it made sense. What was harder was Cathy and Gore? I could only imagine that you didn't believe Chuck when he told you about Gore."

"I didn't. He never let go of Sebastian. It was always there in the back of his mind. He was very jealous and very suspicious. I thought it was a fantasy he had made up to justify what he had done to Sadie. After he was gone and I had moved, I put it out of my mind."

"But when we turned up, you had to make sure. Especially after Patrick put us onto Sebastian. So it was imperative for you to find out if it was true."

"Yes."

"And when you found out it was, you recruited Cathy to help you. You installed Gore in your house and asked her to look after him while you saw to something. And you stabbed her in the back of the neck. There will be a palm print from her forehead."

She shook her head. "I wore a latex glove."

"And you killed her because she was a loose end that could lead us to you. And Gore, because you realized then that what Chuck had told you was true, and it was he, ultimately, who had caused all this. He had been the one, really, who had killed Sadie and Chuck and brought about the ruin of your family. Your own son. The son you could never have with Chuck."

"Yes."

"Your plan was, what? To persuade Sebastian to go away with you? To hide you . . . ?" I laughed. "No, of course not. He was going to be the scapegoat who took the rap for the murders."

She shook her head. "No, not really. First I was going to marry him, in Canada, and then I was going to let you have him. It almost worked." She turned and looked at Dehan with dull eyes. "You almost killed him. If he'd drowned your partner, and you'd killed him, it would have worked."

Dehan screwed up her brows, then narrowed her eyes and stood.

"Angela Inglewood, I am arresting you for the murders of

Chuck Inglewood, Cathy Byrne, and Jonathan Copes. You have the right to remain silent, but anything you do say can be used against you in court of law. You have the right to an attorney, and you have the right to have an attorney with you during questioning. If you cannot afford a lawyer, one will be appointed for you if you wish. If you decide to answer any questions now, without a lawyer present, you have the right to stop answering at any time." She finished up by slapping the cuffs on her and snarling, "You're under arrest!"

To me she shook her head and said, "Come on, genius. Let's get you home."

EPILOGUE

It was just after three in the morning as we made our way down the stairs from the chief's office. We stopped at the door of the detectives' room and I stared in. It was mainly dark, with a couple of guys hunched over desks, in small pools of lamplight. Behind me I heard Dehan say, "I can't believe you saw that so early on. There was no blood on the floor, therefore her alibi was false, therefore she killed him."

I nodded and said, absently, "Which made it likely he had raped Sadie."

I walked into the room, through the darkness, toward the desks we shared. She was leaning on the doorjamb.

"So that made it interesting to get his blood tested for AIDS."

"Yes."

"That's very cool, Stone."

I reached down and opened her laptop. It was still on from the last time she had sat at it, when I had explained the case to her. It seemed like weeks ago, but it was just a couple of days. The light from the screen flooded the desk. I heard her voice from the door.

"Hey! What are you doing?"

She drew closer a few steps and stopped.

It was an article. There was a large, high-definition photograph of a baby in a womb. The title was, BABY'S FIRST WEEKS.

I closed the lid and went to her and put my arms around her. "Anything you want to tell me?"

She held me and leaned her head on my shoulder. "No, I was just daydreaming."

"Well, I am concussed and bruised and dressed in a much bigger man's clothes. I am also badly in need of a third, large whiskey. So I think you should take me home and tell me all about your daydreams."

From down in among the shadows Mo's voice came to us: "Ah, get a room, will ya!"

And we made our way out into the wee, small hours, to the old burgundy Jag, and home.

Don't miss DEAD AND BURIED. The riveting sequel in the Dead Cold Mystery series.

Scan the QR code below to purchase DEAD AND BURIED.

Or go to: righthouse.com/dead=and-buried

NOTE: flip to the very end to read an exclusive sneak peak...

DON'T MISS ANYTHING!

If you want to stay up to date on all new releases in this series, with this author, or with any of our new deals, you can do so by joining our newsletters below.

In addition, you will immediately gain access to our entire *Right House VIP Library*, which includes many riveting Mystery and Thriller novels for your enjoyment!

righthouse.com/email

(Easy to unsubscribe. No spam. Ever.)

ALSO BY BLAKE BANNER

Up to date books can be found at:
www.righthouse.com/blake-banner

ROGUE THRILLERS
Gates of Hell (Book 1)
Hell's Fury (Book 2)

ALEX MASON THRILLERS
Odin (Book 1)
Ice Cold Spy (Book 2)
Mason's Law (Book 3)
Assets and Liabilities (Book 4)
Russian Roulette (Book 5)
Executive Order (Book 6)
Dead Man Talking (Book 7)
All The King's Men (Book 8)
Flashpoint (Book 9)
Brotherhood of the Goat (Book 10)
Dead Hot (Book 11)
Blood on Megiddo (Book 12)
Son of Hell (Book 13)

HARRY BAUER THRILLER SERIES
Dead of Night (Book 1)
Dying Breath (Book 2)
The Einstaat Brief (Book 3)
Quantum Kill (Book 4)
Immortal Hate (Book 5)
The Silent Blade (Book 6)
LA: Wild Justice (Book 7)

Breath of Hell (Book 8)
Invisible Evil (Book 9)
The Shadow of Ukupacha (Book 10)
Sweet Razor Cut (Book 11)
Blood of the Innocent (Book 12)
Blood on Balthazar (Book 13)
Simple Kill (Book 14)
Riding The Devil (Book 15)
The Unavenged (Book 16)
The Devil's Vengeance (Book 17)
Bloody Retribution (Book 18)
Rogue Kill (Book 19)
Blood for Blood (Book 20)

DEAD COLD MYSTERY SERIES
An Ace and a Pair (Book 1)
Two Bare Arms (Book 2)
Garden of the Damned (Book 3)
Let Us Prey (Book 4)
The Sins of the Father (Book 5)
Strange and Sinister Path (Book 6)
The Heart to Kill (Book 7)
Unnatural Murder (Book 8)
Fire from Heaven (Book 9)
To Kill Upon A Kiss (Book 10)
Murder Most Scottish (Book 11)
The Butcher of Whitechapel (Book 12)
Little Dead Riding Hood (Book 13)
Trick or Treat (Book 14)
Blood Into Wine (Book 15)
Jack In The Box (Book 16)
The Fall Moon (Book 17)
Blood In Babylon (Book 18)
Death In Dexter (Book 19)
Mustang Sally (Book 20)

A Christmas Killing (Book 21)
Mommy's Little Killer (Book 22)
Bleed Out (Book 23)
Dead and Buried (Book 24)
In Hot Blood (Book 25)
Fallen Angels (Book 26)
Knife Edge (Book 27)
Along Came A Spider (Book 28)
Cold Blood (Book 29)
Curtain Call (Book 30)

THE OMEGA SERIES
Dawn of the Hunter (Book 1)
Double Edged Blade (Book 2)
The Storm (Book 3)
The Hand of War (Book 4)
A Harvest of Blood (Book 5)
To Rule in Hell (Book 6)
Kill: One (Book 7)
Powder Burn (Book 8)
Kill: Two (Book 9)
Unleashed (Book 10)
The Omicron Kill (Book 11)
9mm Justice (Book 12)
Kill: Four (Book 13)
Death In Freedom (Book 14)
Endgame (Book 15)

ABOUT US

Right House is an independent publisher created by authors for readers. We specialize in Action, Thriller, Mystery, and Crime novels.

If you enjoyed this novel, then there is a good chance you will like what else we have to offer! Please stay up to date by using any of the links below.

Join our mailing lists to stay up to date -->
righthouse.com/email
Visit our website --> righthouse.com
Contact us --> contact@righthouse.com

facebook.com/righthousebooks
x.com/righthousebooks
instagram.com/righthousebooks

EXCLUSIVE SNEAK PEAK OF...

DEAD AND BURIED

CHAPTER 1

Death was there. It was a palpable presence in the dark air.

Virgil Place, just south of Lafayette in Castle Hill, was a quiet, gloomy street, draped with orange light that drooped listless from cold, steel lamps bolted to old wooden telegraph poles. The houses, in funereal ranks, stood dark, with blind windows and silent doors which saw no evil and spoke no testimony.

The houses stood dark, all but number 2242. There, light flooded from the open door and bathed two patrol cars, parked with their red lights pulsing against the blacktop and the walls of the houses around them. There were also two ambulances and a crime scene van, and Frank the ME's beaten-up Ford.

I killed the engine of my old Jaguar, and Dehan pushed open the door. We ducked under the tape, and I stood a moment looking at the house. It was tall, narrow, and brown. The first floor and the upper floor were clapboard, and the basement, which rose about six feet above the ground, was faced in stone. The overall effect managed to combine sinister and grotesque in a way that was not easy.

To the right of the bow window, stone steps rose to a wooden door that stood open, allowing light to stream out onto the front yard and the street, casting shadows of plane trees and pin oaks across the asphalt. Light came also from the window, but the drapes had been pulled closed, so only thin gashes seeped out.

Dehan had stopped at the foot of the steps and was watching me with eyes that were still sleepy. There was a hint of a smile, but she hid it well.

"You solved it already?"

I glanced at her a moment and nodded.

"It was the butler. He did it in the ballroom with Miss Scarlet."

She turned and made her way up the steps, speaking over her shoulder.

"That butler is a hound dawg!"

The cop on the door nodded at us.

"Good morning, Detectives. Down in the cellar."

The house was standard 1930s. There was an entrance hall with stairs rising on the right to the upper floor, a passage leading to a kitchen in back, and a door on the left that led into a long living room and dining room. There was light coming from the upper floor, there was a lot of light coming from the living room, and, along the passage that led to the kitchen, there was a cellar door, and I could see there was light there too. I stopped and spoke to the uniform on the door.

"Was it you who responded to the 911?"

"Yes, Detective. Me and Gunther."

"All these lights were on when you arrived?"

"Yup, door was open like it is now. The light was on in the living room. Lights were on upstairs, and the cellar door was open, also with the light on. Just like it is now."

I nodded. "Thanks." I peered into the living room, muttering to Dehan, "That's a lot of light for one murder."

The living room was dusty. The armchairs and the sofa were expensive, over the top, overstuffed and in white leather. And old. They reeked of the '80s. They were arranged around a brass-and-glass table that had the stench of bad taste and padded shoulders.

The table at the far end had the same stench. It was a slab of inch-thick glass on a Greco-Roman stone pedestal. It also had a film of dust over it. Books on bookshelves that had been built into the alcoves to either side of the fireplace were an eclectic mix of hardbacks and paperbacks. I took in Tutankhamun, Plato, Carlos Castaneda, Agatha Christie, and Anais Nin at a quick look. I didn't see any plants or photographs.

At my shoulder, Dehan said, "Those are vinyls, and that's a record player."

I glanced at her, then followed her gaze. It was focused on a shelf, with maybe five or six hundred vinyl records to either side. The only one I could identify was *Sgt. Pepper's Lonely Hearts Club Band*.

Dehan hissed through her teeth and shook her head. "You don't think about nostalgia being nostalgic, but here it is, the eighties mooning over the sixties."

"In 2020. I wonder if it means anything."

She put a hand on my shoulder and smiled. "Everything means something, big guy."

She made her way to the cellar door, and I followed but took a quick detour to peer in at the kitchen. The lights were on there too.

The steps down to the cellar were narrow and made of bare concrete. The floor, nine steps down from the hall, was also concrete. But roughly at its center there was a hole, five or six feet long and about three feet wide. Arranged around the hole were Frank, the ME, Joe, the head of the crime scene team, one of his guys dressed in spaceman suits, and a platinum blonde in her midthirties, wearing a pretty red dress and high-heeled shoes to match. She was on her back, staring at the ceiling like it had astonished her somehow. She had two ugly wounds in her chest, and underneath her there was a large pool of blood that was still liquid, though it looked like it was beginning to congeal. By her side there was a spade.

Frank glanced at us and then back at the corpse.

"You're early. I thought you two only did cold cases. No one has failed to solve this one yet. You need to come back in about six months."

Dehan jerked her head at the spade.

"Was she digging the scene?"

Frank stared at her while she frowned into the hole in the floor. "That was in remarkably bad taste, Carmen."

She was still frowning at the contents of the hole when she answered, absently, "Yeah? You should see the living room upstairs. That really is in bad taste." After a moment she added, "Man."

I stood by her side and peered in. The hole was occupied by another body, though there wasn't much left of it. By the clothes it looked like a man, but most of the flesh had rotted away, and what hadn't rotted had become hard and leathery. Dehan said, "Corduroy jacket, flared pants, and that looks like a very wide tie."

Frank was still engaged with the platinum blonde. "I haven't got to him yet."

I grinned at Dehan. "Can you at least give us a time of death?"

He stared at me, genuinely shocked. "Oh, that's funny. That's very funny."

Dehan snorted a small laugh and muttered, "Asshole." Then to Frank, "Who is she?"

"No idea. No purse, no papers, nothing." He stood as a gurney rattled down the steps. "We'll see if we get a hit on her DNA or her prints."

I grunted. "Well dressed, tasteful, and in those heels. She didn't come here to do a spot of digging."

Dehan took a couple of pictures of her. Joe looked up from where he was hunkered over the spade, fitting it into a large plastic bag.

"The spade has what looks like fresh earth and concrete on it." He pointed at the edge of the hole. "And the chip marks and scratches look pretty fresh too."

I nodded and squatted down beside him to look at the edges

of the hole. He added, "No way of knowing how fresh, but days rather than weeks."

I looked up at Dehan and sucked my teeth. We stared at each other a moment, and she said, "So she came here to look at the hole, not to make it. Somebody else was making it."

I gave my head a small, sideways twitch that meant "maybe." "Or she was brought here to be shown it. Assumptions, but pretty safe ones, I'd say."

Frank snorted and smiled at Joe. "So that's how he does it. I've often wondered."

Joe chuckled as he stood with the bagged spade. "I've often wondered what a safe assumption was. Now I know. It's truly an education to see the master at work."

Dehan told them to take a hike, then scratched her head as she looked around the gloomy cellar. "So all the lights are on in the house, most of them, anyhow . . ."

I said, "So there was activity in the house, all over the house. We need to confirm that with the neighbor who called it in, that there are not normally this many lights on at night, or so much activity. But on the face of it, it looks like there was a lot of coming and going."

Frank climbed carefully down into the hole while we watched the gurney bearing the blonde's body clunk laboriously up the cellar steps. Dehan spoke absently, to herself.

"She came here to see something, or she came here for somebody to show her something." She blinked and turned to me. "We need to look at the rooms upstairs."

I gave my head a single nod. "To see if there has been a search. I agree." I jerked my chin at the floor. "It's been swept to conceal footprints. With that broom." I pointed at it in the corner, and Joe turned to look at it.

"Got it. We'll check it for prints."

I turned to Frank in the shallow grave. "But, who's this guy? He probably has no ID in that corduroy jacket of his, but what can you tell prima facie?"

I squatted down again, and Frank leaned over, gently feeling the corpse's pockets. Dehan said, "You know, Frank, I always wanted a partner who said things like 'whom' and 'prima facie.' It's what you expect from a homicide cop in the Bronx. Prima facie."

"You two do my head in. Nothing in his breast pockets." He spoke as he worked, "I can't imagine what it's like at home when you're not at work. Constant madness and intellectual rambling. Nothing in his hip pockets. My guess is the killer took it. He was methodical and cool." He glanced at me. "She used to be a nice, bright girl, John, and then you took her and made her like you. Nothing in his pants. Nothing in any of his pockets. No keys, no cash, nada."

I grunted. "What is he, forty?"

Frank sighed, like he was tired of hearing that question. "You know I can't answer that till I get him to the lab . . ."

I ignored the sigh and went on. "Okay, Frank, not more than not less than. He's not one and he's not a hundred. So close the gap for me. He's not twenty and he's not eighty . . ."

"Fine! He's not thirty-five and he's not sixty. That's as close as I'd like to get. A *big* margin of error either side of forty-five. On the face of it—prima facie, as you would say—he seems to have all his own teeth, hair was abundant and seems to be dark brown or black, clothes seem to be early eighties . . ." He inched around to look at the corpse's shoes. "Shoes look expensive. That's about all I can tell you, except that he was about six foot and male. Anything else will have to wait until I have examined him. Now let me work. I'll call you. Goodbye."

I looked at Dehan and made a face. "Sometimes, with Frank, he makes you feel unwanted. I don't know why."

Dehan shook her head and sucked her teeth. "Hold on with an open hand, Stone. He'll come back. Let's go up."

We left Frank sighing and Joe chuckling and climbed the stairs back to the ground floor. Dehan made for the stairs, but I wandered back down the corridor to the kitchen and peered in again. The light was on; there were a couple of cups on the draining board, plus a plate and a glass.

I stood staring at it a minute, then went back along the passage and stood in the living room doorway, with my hands stuffed in my pockets. Dehan hovered on the first step a moment, then dropped back down, came over to stand next to me, looking over my shoulder, and breathed in my ear, "Feeling nostalgic for your teens?"

"The eighties were not a great decade, Dehan." I stepped into the room and stood looking down at the vaguely grotesque sofa and armchairs. "I always wished I had been fifteen in 1965."

She leaned on the doorframe and frowned at me.

"Why fifteen? What happened in 1965?"

"Not a lot, aside from the first combat troops arriving in Vietnam, but it would have meant I was seventeen in '67, the Summer of Love, and I would have been eighteen and nineteen in '68 and '69 respectively. Which might have been fun." I shook my head. "When was the last time, do you think, that a person actually sat in this room and opened one of those books?"

She crossed the floor and stood in front of one of the bookcases, examining the tomes.

"There's a lot of undisturbed dust," she said. Then she turned to the drapes that hung across what I assumed were French doors onto the backyard. She peered through them a moment, then yanked them back and, using a slim flashlight from her pocket, examined the bolts that held the left-hand door to the jamb, top and bottom.

"Gunged up and rusted, and the lock is rusted too. No sign of scrapes or scratches."

I moved to a sideboard where there was a vase. When I lifted it, it left a clear ring in the dust, and inside it were the dried, rotted remains of some kind of organic material.

Dehan said, "I don't think this room has been disturbed for years."

I put down the vase and picked up a lamp in both hands,

looking at the ring it had left. "So what are we looking at, Dehan?" I put the lamp down. "Lay it out for me."

"No. Let's look upstairs first."

I wagged a finger at her. "There is a bathroom where we shall find toothpaste, barely used, and a single toothbrush. There will be minimal, basic toiletries. Three of the four bedrooms will have bare, unmade beds, empty or nearly empty closets, and about as much dust as this room has, but one of them will show signs of having been occupied by somebody with very basic, limited needs. My guess is that Joe might find traces of concrete and dirt in that room."

She stared at me for a long moment. "It's strange," she said. "When you do that, it makes me hot, but at the same time I want to slap you."

"Ja voll," I said, propelling her toward the stairs, "das is your Electra complex vontingk to kill unt luff at zee same time zee superior farzer figure."

"Now I only want to slap you."

Upstairs we found a bathroom and four bedrooms. The bathroom showed signs of minimal use, with a single, almost unused tube of toothpaste and a toothbrush. Dehan grunted at it, like she had expected more of it and it had let her down somehow.

"Whatever DNA we get from that will be ninety percent toothpaste."

She opened the cabinet, pulled out a hairbrush, and scowled at it. I frowned too. The strands of hair in it were long and blond.

"That doesn't make a lot of sense."

"No, Little Grasshopper, you mean it doesn't fit with the sense you are trying to make."

"It makes sense to you? Long blond hair makes sense to you? How?"

I shook my head, then shrugged. "A Hells Angel? She's got long blond hair. Let's look at the bedrooms."

It was pretty much what I had expected. The master bedroom and the two larger rooms had the mattresses wrapped in plastic sheets, the drapes closed, and a strong smell of mustiness, like the doors had not been opened in a long time. The drawers were largely empty, though some had bits of bedding in them that looked, felt, and smelled old and musty. The wardrobes were empty too.

The fourth room was smaller, the bed was made, and, as I had expected, there were noticeable remains of dirt and concrete on the floor, and particularly beside the bed.

Dehan stared around the room awhile, but it had little more to tell us.

"Okay," she said, "you predicted this. What does it mean?"

I rubbed my chin and offered her a smile that was more like a wince.

"It means there was somebody digging a hole downstairs."

"Don't be a wiseass, Stone."

"You didn't look in the kitchen."

"Okay, so what did you see in the kitchen?"

"Two cups, one plate, and one glass."

"So somebody was camped out here, digging a hole. Somebody else came to visit, had coffee, and got killed."

"Thumbnail sketch, yeah. But, question: How long does it take to dig a hole?"

She pulled down the corners of her mouth and hunched her shoulders.

"You have to break the concrete..."

"To do that you need a drill or a pickaxe."

She blinked a couple of times. "Right. Where is it?"

I stared down at the bed, trying to visualize the person who had slept in it. I spoke aloud, to nobody in particular.

"A man dies, presumably murdered, some time back, possibly as much as thirty-five or forty years ago. Somebody dumps his body in a shallow grave in the basement of this house and covers it in concrete. Years go by, maybe decades..."

My eyes drifted from the bed and then met Dehan's. We

stared at each other a moment. I said, "There has to be a record of this guy's disappearance. We need somebody on it."

She nodded and took up where I had left off. "Then, very recently, somebody moves into the house where his body had been hidden. Somebody with long, blond hair. Our Jane Doe? They are camping here, not living. And they don't start digging straightaway. They seem to be doing something else, we don't know what. Eventually, though, they dig a hole in the basement and find John Doe's body. But they don't pull it out or call the cops. They call Jane Doe, who shows up in a pretty red dress and heels. They have coffee, they take her down to the cellar, show her the body, and shoot her. Then they leave, taking the pickaxe with them, but leaving the spade, and all the traces of their having been here, including the toothbrush, plate, cup, and glass. Stone . . ."

"Seen this way it doesn't make a lot of sense."

"You're not kidding. Let's tell Joe to have a look up here, then we'll go talk to the neighbor. What was his name?"

CHAPTER 2

"Mr. Frederick Garner?"

The red lights from the patrol cars pulsed on his face, making him look slightly diabolical. But when you looked more closely, he had prissy lips tightly pressed together, which, with his hands clasped over his belly on his doorstep, made him look more like a prim, disapproving daemon. He gave his head a little waggle and said, "Yes. You'd better come in. I made coffee, but it's probably cold by now." He turned and walked away into the hallway. "I was expecting you about an hour ago, to tell you the truth. I can make some more . . ."

We followed. Dehan answered.

"Thanks, but we won't take much of your time. A uniformed officer will be over later to take a detailed statement."

He led us through the hallway to what looked like a Hollywood depiction of a Victorian parlor. It had walls papered in blue-and-white stripes, wall lamps with elaborate glass shades, burgundy carpets, burgundy armchairs with white lace doilies, and shelves bearing many small statues of girls with long dresses, hats, and parasols.

He sat perched on the edge of the sofa, and Dehan and I each took an overstuffed chair. Dehan spoke.

"Could you walk us through what happened, Mr. Garner?"

He regarded her a moment with arched eyebrows.

"You want me to walk *you* through it now and then give your uniformed officer a detailed statement later. Is there anybody *else* you'd like me to tell about it? I mean, I have only been waiting two and a half hours to talk to somebody. And it *has* been a little traumatic!"

Dehan made a sympathetic face. "Only the judge and the jury when it goes to trial, Mr. Garner. We are very grateful, it's just that everyone has been very busy with, uh, you know, the dead bodies and things."

He caught the sarcasm and turned to speak at me.

"It was two a.m. and I couldn't sleep. Tinker Bell couldn't sleep either. She was up and about and all over the place . . ."

Dehan said, "Tinker Bell?"

He answered without looking at her. "My Burmese cat. I was going to call her Smoky, because she is like a little cloud of silent gray smoke, but Graham said it made her sound like a mackerel, and Misty was *so* corny, so I went for something completely different and settled on Tinker Bell."

"A good choice."

"How would you know? You haven't even seen her. Anyway, Tinker Bell was hyperactive and mewing incessantly. I am sure she could sense something coming. I got up several times to look out of the window, and I could see there was light pouring out of the house next door."

I asked, "What made you look out the window?"

He sort of sagged and sighed at the same time, rolling his eyes to look up at the ceiling.

"It's actually a good question, and the answer is I am not *entirely* sure. However, before you go accusing me of being a nosy parker, the fact is there *were* a couple of shouts, and before that there was the sound of a car arriving, then driving away, feet walking on the sidewalk, doors banging. Nothing, taken in *isolation*"—he leaned forward to give the word emphasis—"nothing that would make you stop and think, 'Oh, my goodness! Somebody is going to get *murdered* tonight.' But taken as a whole, there was an edginess to the night. And of course cats are *so* much more sensitive than you or I."

I nodded like I had noticed that myself. "So when you looked out of the window you noticed a lot of light coming from the house next door."

"Yes."

"Was that very unusual?"

"Oh, heavens yes! You don't see a soul in that house from one month to the next. It's a crying shame when you think that there are people sleeping rough in the parks because they have nowhere to live."

Dehan took a breath, held it, and creased the corners of her eyes.

"Yeah, getting a job can often solve that kind of problem. So, on those rare occasions when the owner of the house did show up, did you ever get to meet him, or her, chat over the fence, have coffee . . . ?"

Garner's face said Dehan was on a slippery slope into hell and he couldn't wait to see her lose her footing.

"We rarely chatted," he said to me, through tight, straight lips. "We were not that well acquainted, but we did exchange pleasantries on occasion."

Dehan asked, "Did he, she, or it have a name?"

"I must say," he said, dilating his nostrils and peering at her down his nose, "I find your manner quite . . ."

"You don't need to like me, Mr. Garner, only answer my questions. What's the owner's name, as far as you are aware?"

"Well, really!" He looked at me, and I shrugged and made a "whatcha gonna do?" face.

"*Her* name is April. April . . ." He thought for a moment. "One of those Scandinavian names, like Olafsen or Amundsen . . . Olsen! April Olsen. She's owned the house for *years*. Ten, fifteen years. Never lived here. I suppose she's from out of town. Always struck me as perfectly respectable. I suppose when she is in town she just pops in and stays at the house. Perhaps it's a pied-à-terre. I mean, how should I know?" He stared at me with wide eyes, like he had suddenly scandalized himself with an outrageous thought. "I am not my sister's keeper, am I? We knew each other to say hello over the garden fence, and comment on the weather."

Dehan found the photograph and showed it to him.

"Is this April?"

He sagged and sighed through his nose.

"Yes. Poor child. Perhaps if I had listened to Tinker Bell and called a little sooner..."

I considered him a moment, wondering how sincere he was, then shook my head.

"You can't hold yourself responsible, Mr. Garner. The only person who is to blame for April's death is the person who shot her."

He didn't look up from the picture.

"It's so hard to know, isn't it? Call too soon and you're a nuisance wasting precious police time, call too late and somebody dies because you were negligent and hesitant." Now he looked up. "Society codifies our behavior, but we take responsibility for it." He smiled, with a hint of nostalgia. "It was easier in the sixties."

Dehan glanced at him with interest. "Yeah? How's that?"

He regarded her with distaste, like she was the spinach he had to eat before he could have his ice cream.

"We didn't have the Hive Mind yet. The big thing now is being 'connected.' The big thing then was being free. Back then you made your choices and you took the consequences. Today we don't see it like that, do we? Society takes the consequences, so society takes the decisions." He held her eye a moment. "I'm saying I should have called the cops sooner, and screw how inconvenient it might be for you or my neighbors."

Something in what he said made me pause.

"She had the house for ten or fifteen years, you said."

"Yes, something like that."

"So I gather you've been here at least that long."

"Much longer. I have been here sixty-five years. I was born in the bed I sleep in now, and shall die in."

"So, who had the house before April did?"

"Oh." He drew back slightly and said again, "Oh, it stood empty for *years*! *Years!* It just stood there, empty."

"How long?"

"Oh, *years*! I don't know how long. Years."

Dehan bit back her irritation and said, "And before that?"

"Oh, my goodness..."

He sat back in the sofa and crossed one leg over the other. Tinker Bell, in the form of a small, gray cloud of fur, jumped up beside him and climbed on his lap. He stroked her absently, staring at the ceiling.

"I mean to say, we are going back, oh ... maybe thirty or forty years. I can't even remember his name. A man, alone. He was divorced as I recall. I know he used to have parties, noisy ones."

"What happened to him?"

He shrugged and made a "how the hell should I know?" face.

"Happened? Nothing happened. He just left, went abroad or something. Whatever, it was a relief. Mommy was ill, poor love, and his parties were a terrible strain on her. After he left, the house stood closed for a long time. Then April started turning up. Sweet kid." His face darkened suddenly, and he turned to me. "That house has *bad* karma, you mark my words."

I grunted and thought for a while. Then I asked him, "Did you see any of the people coming and going last night?"

He shook his head. "No, not at all."

I went to stand, but Dehan said, "Mr. Garner, were you aware of any connection between April Olsen and the previous owner?"

He looked startled. "None at all, except that she must have bought the place from him, of course. But aside from that, not at all. I mean, they are separated by years, aren't they! He would be an old man by now."

She nodded once. "I guess he would." She put her hands on

her knees and glanced at me. I made a face that said I had no more questions, and we stood.

"Thank you for your time, Mr. Garner. As I said, an officer will come over later for your statement."

We stepped out into that darkest hour before the dawn and stood a short while on the sidewalk. We watched the gurney, with the soulless, dehumanized remains of what had once been a man, rattle down the path and get lifted, little more than a sack of bones, into the back of an ambulance.

Dehan jerked her chin at him. "You figure that's the previous owner?"

I made a face that was doubtful. "It's either him or somebody he didn't like much."

She grunted and nodded, then looked at her watch.

"Five thirty. Not much we can do for another three hours. What say we go home, have some breakfast, and chew the cud?"

"Sounds like a plan."

I stood a moment, looking at the yellow sheen of pallid light on the blacktop by the meat wagon, where the shadow of my ancient, burgundy Jag lay hunched, like a cat about to pounce, and Dehan, tall and slender, stood with her elbow on the roof, where the yellow lamplight reflected on her face. She was watching me. She smiled.

"You coming? Or are you going to stand there till the sun comes up?"

My footsteps were loud in the predawn dark. I opened the driver's door and climbed in, left the door open with one foot on the road. She got in next to me and slammed hers. I said:

"I want the financials for April Olsen." Then, "Why'd she buy the house?"

Dehan chewed her lip. I went on.

"She bought the house that she would eventually be killed in. She bought the house with a body buried in the cellar, under solid concrete." I tapped a tattoo on the wooden steering wheel. "She bought a house which, for years, she never really used for anything. If she wasn't going to live in it, she could have let it, or sold it, or advertised it on Airbnb. But she did none of those things. She sat on it and visited occasionally. Then, somebody . . ." I hesitated. "Somebody who wasn't wearing expensive high heels and a pretty dress dug up the corpse in her cellar, showed it to her, and shot her." I stared out at the gloomy street with its unhappy lamplight, then turned to Dehan, where that light looked beautiful laid across the planes of her face. "So for what purpose did she buy that particular house?"

Dehan shook her head. "I know right now you are all about asking the right questions in the right way. But what I think will help a lot more in formulating the right questions right now is four eggs, half a pound of bacon, rye toast, and a gallon of strong black coffee."

I pulled in my foot and let the door swing closed, turned the key in the ignition, and heard the big old engine growl.

"Once again, Dehan, you are right. And wise."

I pushed the stick shift into first and pulled away, accelerating steadily through second and third to fourth gear. We turned right onto a desolate Castle Hill Avenue and hit the gas going north, through Unionport, toward East Tremont.

After five minutes Dehan spoke suddenly.

"Okay, here's one. Was the body the reason she was killed?"

I nodded. "That's a good question. If we can positively connect her with the corpse in the shallow grave, that narrows our pool of suspects to somebody connected to them both."

"Probably."

I nodded. "Probably."

"The obvious question, which follows directly from that one . . ."

"Is, were they killed by the same person? Which leads inevitably to, was she looking for the corpse?"

She shook her head. "No. Somebody *else* was looking for the corpse, found it, and killed her. Besides, it's too pat. And it's full of holes."

"Like?"

"Like, A, how many years did she have the house before digging up the basement? Like, B, why the hell did she wait for somebody else to dig up the basement and then take *her* to see it? *In her own house!* Like, C, going back to what you said earlier, she buys the house and then doesn't use it. If she bought the house with the intention of looking for the guy who was buried in her cellar, why the hell did she never go to the house?"

We were quiet for a while, with only the hiss of the tires on the asphalt and the occasional car passing southbound to break the silence. I spun the wheel and crossed East Tremont onto Bronxdale.

"The fact is, Dehan, from the little we know so far, her behavior in relation to the house does not . . ." I grinned at her. "*Prima facie*, suggest somebody engaged in a desperate, life-and-death search."

"No." She pinched her ear and rubbed the lobe with her thumb. "Like you said, on the very little information we have so far. But, even so, the way she was dressed . . ."

"She had come from somewhere."

"Garner said there was a lot of activity, car doors, lights, people walking . . ."

I grunted and turned right onto Morris Park Avenue.

"Did they arrive together? That would mean . . ." I sighed. "Her killer is camped out in her house, looking for the corpse, he finds it, then arranges to meet her, at a restaurant or something, then brings her back, they have a row that involves storming all over the house, wind up in the basement, and . . . *bang*!"

She puffed out her cheeks and blew air.

"That makes some kind of twisted sense, I guess. It also begs the question—*all* these scenarios beg the question—what was it about him that made it so important to find his body?"

I slowed to turn onto Haight Avenue.

"And having found it, kill her and leave both bodies to be found. Along with all the killer's DNA and fingerprints in the bathroom and the bedroom." I pulled up outside our house, then killed the engine and the lights and sat staring out the windshield, down the long, quiet road. "That is very bizarre behavior, Dehan. I don't think I have ever seen anything like it. We need her financials. I want to know . . ."

She gently punched my shoulder with her right fist.

"Coffee," she said, "you want to know coffee, and bacon and eggs and toast. And then we'll request her financials and everything else. Then everything will make sense. You'll see."

CHAPTER 3

THE COFFEE AND THE BACON DIDN'T HELP, BUT, BACK at the station house, getting on the phone and doing some research did. Dehan leaned back, ran her fingers through her hair, and said, "The property register lists the owner of 2242 Virgil Place as April Olsen, just like Garner said. She bought it from one Marie Braun in 2010. Marie Braun had, in turn, inherited it in 1992 from the previous owner, an Allan Bernstein, who had inherited it twelve years before that from his parents, Saul and Rebeca."

I wagged a pencil between my fingers for a moment.

"So the man Garner had talked about, who kept throwing noisy parties, was Allan Bernstein. Does that make the woman who inherited it and sold it to April Olsen his wife?"

"We should find out. What about you?"

"April Olsen has no listed next of kin except for her parents."

She frowned. "Really? At, what was she, thirty-five? That's unusual."

"Thirty-six. Unmarried, no kids. Her parents are Olsen and Olsen, a firm of civil rights attorneys in DC. I tried calling a couple of times but I just get the answering service. They're in the office from ten a.m."

She snorted. "I like the hours for fearlessly defending the rights of the marginalized and underprivileged."

"Yeah." I glanced at my watch. "I'll give them another try in ten minutes. We should go and see them. I don't want to give them that kind of news over the phone. Aside from that, I'd like to get a handle on April Olsen. Maybe they can tell us what the deal was with that house."

She nodded. "We should also go talk to Marie Braun about her benefactor." She thought for a moment. "We have to be careful. We don't know if the guy in the cellar was her benefactor or her benefactor's victim, or had nothing at all to do with her benefactor. We also don't know if her benefactor was her ex, her brother . . ." She shook her head. "We don't know what that relationship was."

I nodded, grunted, chewed my lip, and went to get some coffee-like liquid from the coffee-like liquid machine. When I got back I put a cup in front of Dehan, dropped into my chair, and picked up the phone. It rang six times, and I was about to hang up when a voice that was educated but trying to sound like a man of the people said, "Yeah, Olsen and Olsen, Greg speaking. What can I do for you?"

"Good morning, Greg, this is Detective John Stone of the New York Police Department. I need to speak to either Mr. or Mrs. Olsen. It is a matter of some urgency."

"Oh, I see. Can I help in any way, Detective?"

"Not unless you are either Mr. or Mrs. Olsen."

"They are not here right now. They usually come in a bit later."

"I'll tell you what we are going to do. I am going to make an appointment with you to see them at four o'clock this afternoon. I'm going to leave New York a little before noon, so I would expect to be in DC before four. I have the office address, so my partner and I will be there at four o'clock or perhaps a little before. Will that be a problem?"

"Well, no, but as I say . . ."

"Just contact them and tell them we're coming and that it is very important. Can you do that, Greg?"

"Yeah, sure, I'll do that. No worries."

He sounded like I had spoiled his cappuccino. I smiled and hung up.

"You think we have time to go and see Mrs. Braun before we head off for DC?"

She was nodding at her computer screen.

"Way ahead of you, big guy." She tossed me a glancing smile. "Joyful Autumns Retirement Home, Waldo Avenue in Fieldstone. That's where I'm going to send you when you start dribbling."

"I'll have fed you to the hounds long before that happens. Where, pray, is Fieldstone?"

"It is a privately owned, affluent neighborhood in Riverdale."

"Our Riverdale?"

"Cross Bronx Expressway, Henry Hudson Parkway, fifteen minutes. The way you drive, maybe fourteen and a half."

"Mad, bad, and dangerous. That's me. It's just her?"

"Apparently, I don't know. There may be a husband and kids." She shrugged. "Let's go find out."

THE JOYFUL AUTUMNS Retirement Home was a converted mansion set among leafy meandering lanes that cocked a well-heeled snook at the grid system, presumably on the grounds that the people who inhabited Fieldstone were far too rich to need to get anywhere in a hurry, much less by means of a boring, straight line. The path of value, the winding, overgrown byways seemed to say, is the one that wends. And I found myself, in my inner being, agreeing with them as I wended my way.

We came at last to the large, Greco-Roman gate that gave access to the short, half-moon driveway and eased in. A flight of granite steps rose to a Georgian doorway that looked down its fine nose at us from beneath a discrete Palladian arch. I killed the engine, and Dehan sat a moment, with her arm resting on the open window, looking up at the grand, elegant entrance.

"Mrs. Braun is clearly not short of cash."

I gave my head a small tilt to one side. "Or at least, whoever is paying for her to be here is not."

She regarded me a moment, pursing her lips, then climbed out of the car. I followed suit, and we ascended the ancient steps to the ancient door.

The entrance hall was the size of a small aircraft carrier. On the left was a long, low counter in dark wood. Behind that were a couple of pretty women with efficient smiles and detached eyes. On the right, the original doors had been removed from what had probably been the ballroom and replaced with institution fire doors that were remarkable for the level of depressing ugliness which they achieved. Ahead, a broad flight of wooden stairs divided into two open ram's horns and rose to a galleried landing on the next floor.

Dehan turned and made her way to the desk and leaned on it with both hands.

"Good morning, I am Detective Dehan, and this is my partner, Detective Stone." She showed the smiling woman her badge. "NYPD. We would like to speak to Mrs. Braun. We called . . ."

"Yes, I remember, you called earlier." The smile didn't falter. "I am not sure how helpful you'll find her."

She stood and came around the counter, and we followed her toward the ugly fire doors. "She has periods where she is quite lucid and charming. She's a highly educated woman, you know. But at other times she is away with the fairies, I'm afraid."

We went through the doors into a room that wasn't so much large as vast. The floor alternated square and round mosaics in a way that must have been either spectacular or nauseating when you were dancing a polka. A series of Greco-Roman columns framed what had once probably been the dance floor and sectioned off the perimeter of the room where you could stand

and drink champagne while you conspired to commit murder and treason. The far wall was all a series of French doors that opened onto a spectacular rose garden with what looked like a genuine Italian Renaissance fountain, only the naked god had no water spouting from his mouth. Or anywhere else, for that matter.

I put my fingers on the smiling woman's elbow to slow her down a little. She turned her smile on me and came almost to a halt.

"Is there any family? Who put her in here? Who pays the bills?"

She spoke softly, as though I was likely to embarrass myself and she was trying to save me from such a fate.

"Um, we don't really inquire into our guests' lives, Detective. But I can tell you that Mrs. Braun's bills are paid from an ample trust fund." She smiled like she'd pulled off a difficult trick. "She is well provided for." She gave a pretty laugh and started to walk again. "As to who 'put her in here'"—she stressed the words, somehow managing to suggest there were inverted commas around them—"nobody 'put her in here.' She chose to reside with us because her mother had before her. She came in with her two daughters, and they visit her regularly, every weekend, like clockwork."

Dehan said, "And Mr. Braun?"

"I'm afraid I have no idea. You'll have to ask her."

We had been walking hesitantly, talking, and now we arrived at a round table beside an open French door. There was a woman seated at it, watching us. She was only in her seventies, but her hair was extremely white and soft and gave her the appearance of being older than she really was. She had very blue eyes, a string of very good pearls, and wore a very fluffy, very pink cardigan. She was watching us with amused, ironic eyes and ignoring the smiling receptionist, who now said, "Mrs. Braun, these are Detectives Carmen Dehan and John Stone, from the New York Police Department. They would like to ask you a few questions."

We were pulling our badges, but she shook her head and waved a hand.

"I don't need to see your credentials. Sit down. I have the early onset of Alzheimer's, chances are in half an hour I won't remember you showed me. I have better periods and worse periods. You're lucky you caught me at a better period right now, but I can't guarantee how long it will last." She grinned at Dehan. "And if my daughters have been up to any kind of shenanigans, I can't promise I won't pretend to be having a bad spell either."

Dehan returned the grin as we sat. "We're not interested in your daughters, Mrs. Braun."

"Of course not. Why should you be? So, in what way do you think I can help you, then?"

I said, "In 1992, you inherited a house in New York."

Her eyebrows rose high on her forehead. "Good Lord! Yes, I did. Was that 1992? It seems like yesterday. What of it?"

"We'd like to know who you inherited it from."

She frowned hard, not trying to remember but trying to understand. "Are you serious? I inherited it from my ex-husband, of course."

I leaned forward, with my elbows on the table. "What was his name?"

"Allan, Allan Bernstein. Don't tell me the bastard has shown up alive! Why, he must be in his eighties by now!"

Dehan glanced at me. I went on, "I am sorry, Mrs. Braun, I know this must be distressing . . ."

"It's not distressing. It's interesting. I want to know what the hell is going on and why you're asking me questions about Allan."

Dehan cut in. "We are a cold-case team, Mrs. Brau . . ."

"Really? You try to solve old cases? How is Allan a cold case? He was a bastard in many ways, but he always honored his obligations."

Dehan went on. "We have a . . ." She hesitated. "We have a set of circumstances which we don't fully understand, and anything you can tell us would be hugely helpful. You said, 'Don't tell me the bastard has shown up alive!' What did you mean by that? How did he die?"

She shook her head. "Well that's just it. He didn't. That is, he may have done. I don't know. He went off to New Mexico to carry out his stupid experiments with mind-altering drugs, as if that hadn't all been done already in the sixties, and then he moved on to Mexico and disappeared. I suppose he found some gorgeous Mexican girl, blew his mind with her, *man*, and got killed by her boyfriend or father or cousin or something. Anyway, after seven years I filed to have him declared dead and I inherited the house and what little money he had left. I already had the trust fund for myself and the kids, and then there are the royalties from the books he wrote. He didn't leave me badly off."

I took a moment to assimilate this. "Forgive me, this may seem like an absurd question, but are you certain that he went to New Mexico?"

"Yes, of course I'm certain. We were divorced at the time of course, and we were not living together, but we stayed in touch and he wrote me from there, and then he telephoned me."

Dehan was screwing up her brow, trying to get a handle on what she was hearing. "He wrote to you and telephoned you. What about?"

Mrs. Braun gave a small sigh through her nose and flopped back in her chair, with her hands in her lap.

"He was such an egotist. He was a brilliant man. He lectured at Columbia in psychology and social sciences, you know? He could have been outstanding, an eminence in his field. But with him it was like with so many artists. What they do is all about *them* instead of the subject. Allan had absolutely *no idea* of the impact he had on the people around him. More to the point, he didn't *care*. That was why I divorced him in the end. I was living with him and so was he. I was just somebody to listen to his theories and hear how brilliant he was. That was bad enough, but when he started throwing crazy, druggy parties and having affairs with young undergraduates, that was the last straw. I packed my bags and left. He couldn't understand it."

Not sure if she had slipped into one of her "not so good" periods, I hesitated. "So, the phone call?"

She laughed. "He tried to tell me that he was researching the impact of mind-altering aphrodisiacs on consciousness. He believed they freed the mind from inhibition and made you more creative. He encouraged me to experiment—him and that friend of his. What was his name? Anyway, I told him experimenting was not just trying things out to see what happened, but developing a theory, from there a hypothesis, and then a set of variables in a controlled environment. Of course it did no good. Even after I had left him he continued to write to me about his ideas, which were increasingly insane, and when he was drunk or stoned or high, he would telephone me. He said I was the only woman he knew who was intelligent enough to understand him. I told him I was the only woman he knew stupid enough to listen to him."

"So when he telephoned you, it was from Mexico . . . ?"

"New Mexico. He wrote to me from Mexico telling me he had been trying peyote buds and he was sure they provided a portal to a parallel reality of the mind. Some such garbage. But he needed the guidance of a shaman to help him navigate that reality. There were none in New Mexico, so he was going to move on to Mexico. A day or so after that he telephoned me and told me the same crap. I told him he was going to lose his place at Columbia. He said he didn't care. He knew he was on the brink of a discovery that would change the world. About a week later he sent me another letter from Mexico, saying he had found the name of an old brujo who was going to guide him in the use of peyote and he was going to write a book about it. That was the last I ever heard from him. I suppose he found some gorgeous Mexican girl, blew his mind with her, *man*, and got killed by her boyfriend or father or cousin or something."

I glanced at Dehan. She had caught the exact repetition too. I figured we didn't have too long.

"Have you any photographs of Allan, Mrs. Braun?"

"No. Why?" She laughed. "Don't tell me the bastard has shown up after all these years!"

I smiled. "No, not as such. Thank you so much for your time, Mrs. Braun. You have been very helpful."

She frowned, and for a moment there was distress in her eyes.

"I have?" And then, "I'm not exactly sure who you are."

Dehan took her hand and smiled. "We were just here to check you were okay," she said. Mrs. Braun smiled back, uncertainly.

"Are you Mexican?"

"A bit?"

"Did you kill Allan?"

"No, that wasn't me."

"Oh, okay. Thanks for looking in."

"You bet."

At the reception desk we paused to ask for Mrs. Braun's daughters' contact details. The woman was still smiling prettily but said, "I can't do that."

Dehan smiled back in the same way and said, "We need to notify them of the death of their father."

"Oh . . . What I *can* do is get them to contact you on an urgent matter. How will that do?"

I told her it would do fine, and we stepped out into the morning sunshine.

Scan the QR code below to purchase DEAD AND BURIED.
Or go to: righthouse.com/dead=and-buried

Printed in Dunstable, United Kingdom